GETTING A
WAY WITH
MURDER

GETTING A WAY WITH MURDER

by

Ralph McInerny

A FATHER DOWLING
Mystery

THE VANGUARD PRESS
NEW YORK

Library of Congress Cataloging in Publication Data

McInerny, Ralph M.
    Getting a way with murder.

    I. Title.
PS3563.A31166G4   1984   813'.54   84-11982
ISBN 0-8149-0894-2

Designer: Tom Bevans.
Manufactured in the United States of America.
        1 2 3 4 5 6 7 8 9 0

*To Miriam and Evelyn Shrifte
for reasons that, like themselves,
are different but related,
this ninth Father Dowling mystery,
with love and thanks*

GETTING A
WAY WITH
MURDER

1

THE TRIAL lasted three days, the jury deliberated less than an hour, the verdict was not guilty.

If the judge and defense attorney, a flamboyant phony named Farrell, were surprised, the defendant was, what? "Disappointed" was the word that occurred to Roger Dowling.

Downs had been asked to stand while the foreman of the jury read the verdict that acquitted him. Then Downs turned slowly, as if testing his unexpected freedom, and his eyes met Roger Dowling's. Met them for a moment, then turned away. Before the priest could take his from Downs the man turned again and now his glance was bright with a sudden fear. The priest lifted a hand in a gesture of reassurance. He did not know if Downs saw it. He had been surrounded by police, apparently on the alert lest this unexpected verdict bring a violent response. A groan had risen from the pewlike seats when the foreman spoke his piece and now there were loud and angry voices around Dowling.

"If that son of a bitch is innocent I'm the Shah of Iran."

"He's dead."

"That's what I mean."

The aspirant to the throne of Persia looked angrily at Roger Dowling when he pressed through; the man seemed to find Dowling's Roman collar a symbol of all that had made the criminal justice system a laughingstock.

■ 9 ■

"I thought we only got forgiven in the next life, Padre." The remark had started off surly, but in mid-expression the speaker seemed to dissociate himself from his own words.

Father Dowling gave the man a small smile and continued to the courthouse corridor. Tuttle stood there, his Irish tweed cap pulled low over his untrustworthy eyes but not enough to erase the expression of naked envy from the little lawyer's face.

"So much for good living, Father Dowling. Farrell hasn't drawn a sober breath since he was assigned the case and he gets the acquittal of the half century."

"It's hardly that much of a coup, Mr. Tuttle."

"It's the biggest surprise in a Fox River court since I passed the bar. Everyone knows he killed her."

"Except the jury."

"The jury!"

Roger Dowling hoped Tuttle's sneering contempt for the jury system was not widespread among members of the bar. But then, it was scarcely fair to take Tuttle as typical, anymore than Peanuts Pianone was a representative policeman. The latter individual, scion of one of the oldest and sleaziest Fox River political families, came shuffling toward them across the polished granite floor, a can of Coke held delicately between the thumb and index finger of one outstretched hand.

"That for me, Peanuts?" Tuttle made an unsuccessful pass at the soft drink.

"Whadya think of the verdict, Tuttle?"

"I'm glad I didn't take the case," Tuttle said, pushing back his hat. There was a rare look of bleak self-knowledge on his face. "I couldn't have gotten him off."

"You think he was innocent?"

Tuttle snapped out of it. "What the hell's that got to do with anything?"

Roger Dowling continued to the great spiral staircase that would take him to street level. How this building echoed! Going down the steps, his gloved hand on the brightly polished brass handrail, Dowling imagined that old cases continued to echo under this cupola until the Last Trump when, as the man had suggested, the final and truly just sorting out would be made. Downs would be acquitted there too, at least of the crime for which he had been tried. He had not murdered his wife. He had told this to Father Dowling and the priest believed him, not least because Downs clearly had not cared whether he was believed or not. He was not exonerating himself. He was not claiming to be poorly treated by society. He would have gladly accepted a guilty verdict and the consequent punishment although he had not murdered Gloria Downs, his wife of many years.

"What I did was worse." Downs smoked incessantly, absent-mindedly. Even when he wasn't smoking he smelled so strongly of tobacco he might just as well have been.

"I took it up again since the murder. Gloria had nagged me into quitting. She said it would add years to my life." A wry smile lifted one corner of his thin-lipped mouth. His face was narrow and the hollow cheeks bore unshaven stubble. Downs was a tall man, six feet three, thin for his height, nondescript except for the clear china-blue eyes and his lean long-fingered hands. It had been difficult not to wonder if those hands had been a murder weapon. "Compared to hers, I guess she was right."

Father Dowling had gone uninvited to talk with Downs. It had been Keegan's suggestion, the captain of detectives controlling the distaste he felt for the defendant. Mrs. Keegan had left Phil prematurely alone. His idea was that the loss of his wife would be sufficient punishment for Downs.

"If he murdered her, he is unlikely to miss her."

"He'll miss her. So they had a little fight."

A little fight did not seem sufficient to explain the condition of the house in which the body of Gloria Downs had been discovered, stabbed nine and a half times and then strangled. The half stab was the coroner's count of the effort that had broken the blade of the knife and apparently decided the assailant on strangulation as the appropriate method of killing.

"Has he asked for a priest?"

"He's not thinking too good."

"How do you even know he's a Catholic?"

"He's wearing a medal."

It was a St. Christopher medal but Downs was not a Catholic. He said he had worn it since a chaplain gave it to him in Vietnam. He had only the vaguest idea who St. Christopher was. Dowling would not have told him that the saint had been stricken from the rolls even if he himself shared the scholarly skepticism of the Bollandists. Dowling took the cigarette offered him. That was when he heard that Downs had reacquired the habit since being accused of his wife's murder.

"Did your wife smoke?"

Downs looked at him for the first time. "I told you she nagged me into quitting."

"That doesn't answer my question."

Downs's smile seemed a signal of gastric distress. "You never met my wife, did you, Father?"

"No."

"You seem to have guessed the kind of . . ." he stopped, but then decided to go on. "The kind of bitch she was. Smoked like a chimney and kept insisting that I quit. I know she expected to outlive me, whatever I did. As an actuarial matter." It was the remark of an insurance salesman, which was what Downs had been, and, given the acquittal, would be again. When the priest said nothing—he had long since learned never to take sides in quarrels between spouses, and the fact that Gloria was dead did not abrogate the rule — Downs murmured, "Frailty, thy name is woman!"

"*La donna è mobile.*"

Downs laughed aloud. Dowling wished he hadn't. It was that single outburst of laughter he remembered later when the weird sequel of the conversation returned to trouble him.

"She was the same about religion."

"Oh?"

"She liked to watch TV preachers, answering them back, sneering at talk of conversions and miracles and all the rest. But she got hooked on them. In her own way she got religion."

"How so?"

"She began to get after me to go to church. Not with her, by myself. That's when she told me she wasn't baptized so none of it applied to her."

Roger Dowling sensed that they had arrived at an important point.

"That's what I was doing with the body in the bathroom. That's how I got blood all over myself."

Downs had called the police to tell them his wife was dead after bleeding all over the place. When the patrol car arrived at the house the door was not answered and, given the nature of the call, the police broke in. They found Downs in the upstairs bathroom, the lifeless body of his wife lying across his knees. He himself was seated on the stool. Water was running in the bathtub and ribbons of blood mingled with the water. It was Horvath who likened the scene to a perverse imitation of the Pietà.

"What were you doing?"

Downs looked at the priest, his expression more distant now, and said matter-of-factly, "I was baptizing her."

■ 13 ■

2

PHIL KEEGAN had watched more sure-fire prosecutions break on the rock of a poorly prepared case, a numskull of a judge, or the contrariness of a jury, to let the Downs acquittal get him down. He invited Horvath across the street to the Florida Bar for a beer. Cy was taking it hard.

"Sometimes I think we could show a film to the jury so they could see A murder B, and they would still acquit."

"Of course they would. The world is mushy and sentimental, Cy. Punishment is out. Maybe we all know we deserve so much of it ourselves we're reluctant to hand it out to others."

It was the kind of stupid remark that appeared in editorials in the Fox River *Messenger* and Keegan was sorry he had added to Cy's despondency with such two-bit philosophy. You had to know Cy as well as Keegan did to find despondency in his expression. The big Hungarian face of the lieutenant had one all-purpose expression and not even the end of the world was likely to change it. Whatever Cy thought of Downs getting off, he certainly didn't think it was the end of the world. It turned out his thoughts had more to do with Agnes Lamb.

The promising, aggravating, accusative, and very black Officer Lamb had appointed herself the conscience of the Fox River Police Department, bent on insuring that whites got the same kind of treatment as blacks. This called for worse rather than better treatment of whites and the Downs acquittal had set Agnes going. Keegan had suggested the Florida as much to get away from her as to console Cy. On his way home he would stop at the St. Hilary rectory for dinner with Father Dowling and no doubt a rehash of the trial. However philosophical he might be with Horvath, Keegan had no intention of encouraging Father Dowling to see crime and punishment as secondary matters.

Those were the exact words he used, as accusingly as Agnes Lamb, when, supper done, they were having coffee, joined at the dining-room table by Marie Murkin, the housekeeper.

"Crime," Roger repeated softly. "If we could use the term only when there is guilt and never when there is not, things might be somewhat different. But you would also have to be sure you knew who are criminals and who are not. You deal at most with a sampling of putative criminals."

Keegan exchanged a look with Marie. Did she know what putative meant? He sure as hell didn't. He wasn't certain he caught the drift of Dowling's remarks at all. Not that the priest was through. He was talking of sin, of course, sin and forgiveness.

"How about sin and punishment?"

"Of course. Eventually. But meanwhile there is always the chance of mercy."

"Well, the judge certainly had mercy on that awful man Downs." Marie had been moving the salt and pepper shakers around as if she were playing chess with the pastor.

"We all need forgiveness. And maybe not just for the crimes we are accused of."

"Crap," Phil Keegan said. "Pardon my Latin. Talk about being caught in the act. Downs was soaked with his wife's blood. His fingerprints were on the knife. The towel she was strangled with had his bloody fingerprints all over it. He did it, Roger. He did it and he got away with it and now why don't we play some cribbage?"

Marie pushed back from the table immediately, welcoming the change of subject. Keegan had noticed that Marie got even more upset than he did whenever he had to cross swords with his old friend. The fact that Dowling had visited Downs as a priest excused his wishy-washiness in this instance. Particularly when Keegan remembered who had asked Roger to go see Downs.

They switched to the cluttered study, three walls of which were lined with books placed every which way in the shelves. The room was sweet with the smell of pipe tobacco and sweeter still with memories of pleasant evenings spent here.

Keegan's wife was dead, his daughters married and living far away, and he had nothing but his job as captain of detectives to keep his mind from the great emptiness at the heart of his life. As a young man, Keegan too had aspired to the priesthood, and he had attended Quigley, the preparatory seminary of the Chicago archdiocese, two years behind Roger Dowling. In that preconciliar church, knowledge of Latin was a sine qua non for a seminarian. Alas, Phil Keegan and the language of Cicero were destined never to become friends. He tried every trick of memorization known, and still the paradigms slipped as easily from his mind as leaves from autumn trees. He left. He had no choice. He went into the service, became an M.P., and found his destiny. After his discharge he joined the Fox River police force and the rest, as he would never have said, is history. He had been widowed a year when Roger Dowling was unexpectedly assigned to St. Hilary's, a parish that had fallen on evil days, the interstates having isolated the parish plant in a triangle bordered by incessant noise. There were few young people left in the parish, the school was closed, the chancery used the assignment as a species of punishment.

Before Roger Dowling arrived, the parish had been intermittently served by a series of Franciscans between assignments. That so distinguished a priest as Roger Dowling should come to this withered plum at the edge of the diocese had been a mystery at first. But Roger had told his old friend quite frankly of his troubles with alcohol — it almost seemed they were trading stories of tragedy, the loss of a wife, Roger's humiliation by drink — but however it had come about, Phil Keegan regarded it as a godsend. He had become a regular visitor to the rectory. He attended Roger's noon Mass most days. And, inevitably, Roger learned of the cases Phil was working on. A mixed blessing that, but sometimes, as in the Downs business, it was good to know he could call confidently on a reliable priest to take a thankless job on short notice. Not that he had asked Roger the outcome of the meeting. Meetings. The priest had gone regularly to Downs's cell. In a way, Keegan was jealous, since Roger knew a good deal more about Downs than the police possibly could. But they knew enough. Downs had murdered his wife. That was a fact, no matter how complicated Roger Dowling might try to make it.

"Did you talk to Downs afterward?"

The priest shook his head. "He was pretty busy and I didn't want it to seem that I was giving my blessing to the verdict. I don't mean my personal blessing..."

"So you do think he was guilty?"

Roger smiled. "Of what?"

"All right," Keegan said angrily. "Maybe you have reasons you don't want to talk about it."

"But we are talking about it. I already told you I don't think he murdered his wife. Insofar as one can know such things, I know he didn't."

"And you have a perfectly easy way to explain the blood all over him?"

"I wonder what the jury made of that?"

"What Farrell told them to."

Farrell, his rhetoric riding the winds of a martini lunch, had painted a vivid picture of Downs returning to his home, finding

■ 17 ■

his wife slain, and then dragging her from the bedroom to the bathroom. He invited the seven women and five men to recall Heathcliff taking the dying Cathy to the window so she could look upon the moors one final time. The expressions of the jury suggested that the allusion was lost on them — Farrell was in his sixties and in his memory Merle Oberon and Laurence Olivier were youthful still — but the pathos of his voice supplied the deficiency in their moviegoing experience. Keegan had seen tears form in several pairs of eyes, and not merely women's, as the jury seemed physically drawn toward the spellbinding Farrell, who could have whispered, the courtroom was so quiet. Perhaps this had been the point when the prosecutor lost his case.

"Downs owes Farrell a lot," Father Dowling said.

"He does indeed. In several senses. His money and his life."

His life. Keegan thought as he had before of the emptiness that stretched ahead of Downs now. However annoying his wife may have been, she had been a companion, and there were times when Keegan believed that any companion at all was better than none. He himself realized how lonely life can be. Downs's motive was supposed to be double: hatred of his wife and the desire to take up with Phyllis Whitmore, the office manager of his insurance firm. Keegan had interrogated Phyllis Whitmore several times, personally, if only to take the pressure of Agnes Lamb's questioning off the woman. Well, that had been what he told Cy. He had been curious to see what truth there might be in the claim that Downs had been running around with Phyllis Whitmore.

She was a tall woman, as tall as Keegan almost, so that made her at least as tall as Downs. Keegan's incredulity had started with that fact. In his view of the world, men did not take up with women who might dominate them physically. It was unnatural, on both sides. Women like to look up to a man, literally; in a way they feel secure at the very threat of male strength since it is there to protect them. Keegan had not liked the way Agnes Lamb smiled during his statement of these home truths.

"Maybe he liked women to beat up on him," she said.

"Look at his wife," Cy added. "I mean the nagging."

"Which is supposed to be a motive for killing her," Keegan said quickly. "You can't have it both ways. If he hated his wife's nagging, he wasn't likely to take up with an Amazon like Phyllis Whitmore."

That word suggested something more than size and that was unfair. Phyllis Whitmore was a most feminine young lady. And she was nervous when Keegan questioned her.

"Did you know Mrs. Downs well?"

"I scarcely knew her at all. She came to the office from time to time and we talked."

"You were never invited to their home?"

"Only on very formal occasions. Mr. Downs had an annual Christmas party at his house and he invited everyone to that. It was a general invitation."

"Then you have been in the house."

"Like everyone else at the office."

"How many are there?"

"Nine. That's everybody, from Mr. Downs to the mail boy."

The agency occupied a building next to the Fox River bank and it was a most impressive layout. From the elevator one entered a spacious reception area with several very large potted trees that, with the hanging plants all about, gave the office an oddly out-of-doors look, pretty good for the fourteenth floor. Machines clacked away among the greenery and a slim girl at the reception desk smiled relentlessly at Captain Keegan. A plaque on her desk indicated that she was Michelle Moran. Her jet black hair was pulled back tightly on her head and this seemed to keep her heavily mascara'd eyes wide and her dark red lips always parted in the smile that would have done well as an advertisement for dental hygiene. Keegan was used to the dimming of smiles when he said who he was, but Michelle Moran went on smiling as if he had made her day when he said he wanted to talk to Phyllis Whitmore. If nothing else, her boss's bereavement should have altered her enigmatic smile.

There were four associates. Associates, not partners. Phyllis Whitmore insisted on it and Keegan got the impression that she would be a stickler for such precisions. It seemed the right trait for an office manager. He didn't have to be told that she was not to be confused with the secretaries, let alone the minor clerical help. All in all, the Downs agency was a bustling concern. It was to emerge in the course of the investigation that Downs was personally worth the better part of two million. It seemed a lot of money to make from selling insurance. Like most people who put a noticeable fraction of their income into insurance, afraid to be without it, Keegan did not really approve of betting that bad luck would strike him and hoping to lose. The vice of gambling and the virtue of insurance, Roger Dowling had murmured. He seemed to be quoting.

"Have you any idea how the Downses got along, Miss Whitmore?"

"Call me Phyl."

"I will not. That's my name."

"Sorry. They hated each other."

"How do you know?"

"Everyone knew. She was a witch. Gene Lane, one of the associates, called her a harridan. Look it up. I did. It fits."

"Do you mean she picked on him in public at their Christmas party?"

"No."

"Did you ever see Mrs. Downs treat her husband badly?"

■ 20 ■

The answer did not come immediately. "No."

"How could everyone know something nobody knew?"

"I heard stories."

"From whom?"

She squared her shoulders and put her hands flat on her desk. "Aren't these peculiar questions?"

"What's peculiar about wanting to know if a man and his wife got along when it looks as if the man killed her?"

"I mean that it's peculiar to ask me. Ask Mr. Downs."

"Oh, we'll be asking everyone, Miss Whitmore."

"Do as you like, Phil." She was being snippy and he knew it, but he liked her for it. He did not intend to bring up then the other thing they had heard, the story of the affair between Downs and Phyllis Whitmore. Something in her manner suggested that she knew he knew, but obviously she wasn't going to bring it up herself. Phyllis Whitmore had been in court the first two days of the trial but was conspicuously absent when the verdict was read.

There had been something between Downs and his office manager. Agnes Lamb came up with pretty conclusive proof, but it was proof to be used in questioning Downs, not Phyllis Whitmore. Downs neither affirmed nor denied the charge.

"Believe what you like, Captain Keegan."

"It's not a matter of belief. You left a pretty obvious trail. Did your wife find out about you and Miss Whitmore?"

You would have thought that possibility had never crossed his mind. By this point, Keegan's sympathy for Downs was wearing pretty thin. Apparently the guy needed the punishment he was sure to get. What brass. Caught with bloody hands, he yet denied he killed his wife. His affair with Phyllis Whitmore was even easier to establish than that he had killed his wife, yet Downs sat there, puffing on a cigarette, treating the suggestion as of little or no consequence.

■ 21 ■

"For God's sake, Downs, it's your *motive*. Can't you see that? With Phyllis Whitmore in his bag of tricks, the prosecutor will have no trouble convincing a jury of what you did."

How certain he had been at the beginning of the investigation. And his certainty had grown as the days went by. When that old fake Farrell was assigned to defend Downs—Downs simply refused to engage counsel and when the judge explained that he would appoint a lawyer, Downs was passive—Keegan had thought the insurance man's fate was sealed. Indeed, for someone who denied having done anything wrong, he seemed almost eager to help the prosecution.

"Did I say I never did anything wrong?"

For a split second, Keegan had thought a confession was in the offing, but Downs was just being enigmatic. Who is innocent? Keegan was sure he heard the echo of Roger Dowling in that question.

"Now he is free to marry Miss Whitmore," Roger Dowling said.

"Ms. Whitmore," Keegan corrected, even as he had been corrected. He wondered if she would take Downs's name or just his money.

The rustling sounds of the cards as Roger Dowling shuffled them brought Keegan's mind back from these thoughts. It was water over the dam now. There wasn't a chance in the world they were going to contest the verdict. Downs was a free man, for what it was worth.

As far as Fox River was concerned, he was a man who had gotten away with murder.

3

IF BEING glad that Downs had been found innocent of his wife's murder was the Christian thing to do, Marie Murkin was not on the side of the angels this time. Not only was she unhappy, she would not have wanted to feel any other way. She didn't make a big thing of it with Roger Dowling, of course. What was the point? If he could empty the jails he would be glad to do it. Maybe that was all right in a priest, but as far as the rectory housekeeper was concerned, Downs should be hanged from the highest tree.

She was sure Phil Keegan felt the same way but she didn't want to seem to be ganging up on Father Dowling. So she let the men go off to the study while she did the dishes. If they could forget Downs with a little game of cards, she could surely do the same washing dishes.

She did them by hand, out of preference. Several times she had threatened to quit her job if Father Dowling bought her a dishwashing machine as he insisted he would.

"I *like* to do them by hand."

"Should we throw out the washing machine too?"

"Clothes are different."

And they were. When she sank her hands into a sink full of hot sudsy water, her flesh smarting against the heat as they disappeared under the fluffy soap, Marie Murkin felt as close to unalloyed contentment as she ever would. For one thing, a sink full of suds and dishes brought back memories. If she closed her eyes, she could imagine herself back in the kitchen at home, her mother there with her—they took turns washing and drying—and the years just melted away and Marie Murkin was a girl again.

She snapped open her eyes. Memories were nice but she didn't want any sentimental nonsense. For another thing, dishes got cleaner when they were done by hand. She didn't have a doubt in the world about this, though her conviction was not founded on any true comparison. All she needed to know was what she knew when she rinsed the just washed dishes and went about drying them, rubbing with great vigor. How could glasses be made to sparkle like this in a machine? And silverware. She wasn't going to risk poisoning the pastor with silverware that was not cleaner than new. Washing dishes by hand has its drawbacks, of course, and thinking about how nice it was to be halfway to her elbows in hot suds invited the accident.

She was rummaging around under the suds when the point of a steak knife nicked her thumb. She slid her hands more deeply into the water, as if ignoring the cut would make it go away, and that was a mistake. Blood from the cut rose upward and suddenly she was looking at a scene too reminiscent of that which had been so lengthily described in the trial. Marie Murkin had only one weakness—the sight of blood, particularly her own. She had fought against it, she had told herself how silly it was, once she had actually gone down to the blood bank intent on donating a pint for one of the parishioners. Already in the waiting room she was jumpy. When the nurse tried to take a sample of her blood by pricking her finger, Marie had keeled over. So, looking at the blood mingling with the soapy water, redder against the white of the detergent, she screamed aloud.

She waited, eyes closed, embarrassed as could be, certain Father Dowling and Phil Keegan would come thundering into the kitchen from the study. They didn't. They apparently hadn't heard her. No one had heard poor Mrs. Downs either when her husband was plunging that knife into her again and again and again....

Marie opened her eyes only after she had pulled the plug and waited for the feel of cool air on her wrists and hands telling her the sink was drained. She wrapped her hand in a dish towel, a huge bandage, like that on a gouty foot in a comic strip. Without looking into the sink, she ran cold water for a full minute, then turned toward the door that led up to her room. She would finish the dishes in the morning. There was a sound behind her. Phil Keegan stood in the doorway.

"Did you make a noise?"

"What kind of a noise?"

"I didn't hear it. Father Dowling thought he heard a scream."

"The house is haunted."

"What's wrong with your hand?"

Marie mutely lifted the bandaged hand. She felt like a puppeteer, speaking to Phil Keegan through a turbaned Turk as dummy.

"I cut myself."

"Your wrists?"

"Aren't you funny. Tell Father Dowling I'm going to bed. You two will have to serve yourselves if you want anything."

"You haven't done the dishes."

For a crazy moment she imagined the two of them finishing up the job she had left undone. Maybe it was thinking of long ago, with her mother, before her life had really begun and she had made the vast mistake of marrying Murkin. How full of hope she had been. She could recall what it had been like sometimes when she was with Phil Keegan. Like now. There was something domestic about the two of them standing here in the kitchen of the St. Hilary rectory.

"They will keep, Captain Keegan. Good night."

The upstairs of the rectory was divided; the pastor's stairway was at the front of the house, hers here in the back, leading up from her kitchen. Marie Murkin mounted the stairs feeling a faint twinge of self-pity, but that was normal. She thanked God for this job and for her lovely room, a diminutive apartment really, but it made her life seem awfully like a nun's. She had the eerie certainty that one night she would die in her bed, there would be a little fuss and a funeral and that would be the end of Marie Murkin. Well, what else did she expect? The Nobel prize for housekeeping? Even that wouldn't keep death from her door. She shook her head impatiently as she reached the top of the stairs. Honestly, the thoughts she was having tonight. Somehow they were due to that stupid verdict in the Downs trial, though she could not have said how.

She did not turn on the switch just inside her door. She found the ceiling light harsh and much preferred to bathe the room in a pinkish glow from the lamp beside her bed. It was a floor lamp that served both the chair and for bedtime reading. All she had to do was turn it over her pillow. If she took care of the rectory in an orderly fashion, Marie Murkin lived according to elaborate ritual in her upstairs abode. It would have been possible to lay out her progress about the room, into the bathroom, out again, chalking footprints on the floor the way actors guide themselves about the stage. Some might find this mechanical. Unconsciously, Marie fought her growing sense of the fragility of life with a routine that anticipated eternity. Unconsciously. All she knew was that she became upset if she altered her routine.

She undressed quickly, in the closet, the door pulled all but closed, and when she emerged it was in nightie and robe and fluffy slippers. But tonight she had had to take care of that darned cut before she could get undressed and this made her nervous and jumpy when she finally slipped into bed. Then she had to get right out because she had forgotten to adjust the lamp. She was almost settled in again before she realized she did not have her book. Her nighttime reading was St. Francis de Sales's *Introduction to a Devout Life*. Once Father Dowling had made a passing allusion to the work as one that was particularly helpful for lay people. The pastor would have been surprised at the consequences of his offhand remark. Probably no one in the world had read St. Francis's *Introduction* more often or more attentively than Marie Murkin. It scared the hell out of her, that book. If it laid out what was ordinarily expected of the Christian, she was in trouble indeed. Her favorite chapters were those at the beginning of the work, where the saint wrote with surprising authority on hell and purgatory. The chapters on heaven were not nearly so convincing to Marie. But if the book frightened her, it was a pleasant fear. She was giving her life to God, in a sense, working here in the rectory, and just fifty yards away, in the church, the Blessed Sacrament was presided over by a flickering red lamp. The thought of Jesus so close gave Marie a nice feeling and added zest to the tremor she felt when she was reading about eternal damnation.

Tonight, because of cutting her finger and getting thrown off schedule, she was truly frightened again by the saint's reminder of the grim stakes of human life. Marie supposed it would drive you nuts if you kept thinking that each and every thing you do adds up to what you are, the way you are likely to remain for all eternity. And there was really no way of being sure how you were doing. Tonight, she bit her lower lip and shivered under the covers and did not spend much time with Francis de Sales. After a page and a half she put the book on the floor, turned off the light, and settled down to sleeplessness.

The awful thing was that, from the moment she put her head on the pillow, she was convinced she would not sleep a wink. She lay there, trying not to think of purgatory and hell, hearing very faintly the voices of Phil Keegan and Father Dowling below. Sleep would not come. She had half a mind to get up and turn on her television. But at this hour there was nothing but what Marie called Dirty Talk Shows, grown-up people sitting around giggling and making suggestive remarks. It was like a playground full of snickering kids.

The sound of the phone lifted her off the bed. She sat up, her heart in her mouth, startled out of her wits. The phone almost never rang this late at night. It did not get through the second ring, meaning that Father Dowling had answered it downstairs. Marie turned on the light, blinked for a moment, and then looked at the phone. She did not have to imagine it was in use. A little light glowed, telling her the phone in the study was open. Trying not to think of what she was doing, Marie eased the receiver off the hook and brought it to her ear.

"Father Dowling?"

"Speaking."

"This is Howard Downs."

"Ah."

"I must see you."

"Certainly."

"I mean right away."

Father Dowling paused and Marie hoped he would tell that murderer to come during the day, like civilized people.

"Of course. I have a visitor but if you came..."

"I'll come immediately."

"Is something wrong?"

A pause. "I have just murdered Vincent Arthur Farrell."

There was a click of a phone and Marie could not muffle her gasp. On the still-open line the pastor spoke.

"As long as you're awake, Marie, you might just as well come down and put on coffee."

4

PHIL KEEGAN had another bottle of beer but switched to the strong coffee Marie Murkin brewed before Downs arrived. Father Dowling had checked with headquarters, blandly asking what was new, and was told nothing about Vincent Arthur Farrell. Father Dowling found that he was not surprised. The urgency in Downs's voice was not due to his fear that Farrell's death would soon be discovered.

"Was the man serious?" Keegan asked.

"We have to assume that."

"Well, I'm going to find out."

"Don't, Phil," Roger said when Keegan reached again for the phone. "Let's hear him out first. For all we know, it may be a joke."

"A joke!"

"Well, maybe not a joke."

"It would be one hell of a joke, is all I've got to say."

"It's on me, if it is, Phil. He didn't know you were here, and nobody else seems to know about it. I am assuming that if someone came upon a body they would phone the police."

"He didn't this time."

Father Dowling let it go. The bizarre outcome of the trial for his wife's murder was one thing. Downs's claim to having killed Farrell, the man who had won his acquittal, was so completely weird that the priest wondered if he had even begun to plumb Downs's personality.

Keegan was spooning sugar into his coffee as Father Dowling carefully filled one of his larger pipes with tobacco. What odd creatures we humans are, he thought. Marie was banging around in the kitchen, trying to pretend she was annoyed at this late-night excitement. Of course she wouldn't have missed it for the world. It seemed important to notice his own and others' idiosyncracies now since he had the feeling it was because Downs owned an insurance agency that he had not really taken the man seriously before.

Had he not, without explicitly formulating the thought, considered the charge against Downs as perfectly compatible with the man's apparent vision of life? On the assumption that Downs had been bent on acquiring wealth, the man had not only attained his goal but learned what a hollow one it was. Money is supposed to bring happiness. Everyone knew and mouthed the words that it did not, but the majority go on acting as if money and true content are one. What is more puzzling than to reach our goal and find it leaves us empty? And what possible intrinsic satisfaction could there be in selling insurance?

There! That was it. Dowling had hit upon the latent attitude he had had in speaking with Downs. The man's life was taken up in an essentially trivial task, persuading people that though they must die, their money could achieve immortality, go on pullulating when they were gone. People spoke of burying their money, but it was its resurrection they counted on. Many years ago a magazine called *Integrity* had been edited for several years by Catholic laypeople, and Roger Dowling had read it avidly. Its articles were exciting examples of drawing out the implications of Christian belief to the point where one became uneasy.

Could logic really entail the consequences drawn in *Integrity*? There had been a whole issue devoted to the concept of insurance. The basic argument was that it was a substitute for Providence by those who had no faith; for Christians to enter into this grisly pari-mutuel was worse than outrageous. Roger Dowling, a seminarian at the time, had found the argument deliciously outrageous. In many ways it was on a par with the view that faith precluded medicine. And why not get rid of housing and any provisions for the morrow? He had been full of refutations as he read—after all, as a seminarian he spent his days acquainting himself with the most serpentine theological argumentations—but at the same time he had had a lurking liking for the outlook. He was reminded of the power of the message of the gentle man from Assisi. Or of Christ himself. Foxes have holes and birds have nests but the Son of Man has nowhere to lay his head. Although Dowling had resisted *Integrity*'s dismissal of insurance, the magazine's view had clearly influenced him. He held no policy on his own life. He had automobile insurance because it was a state law. Did he at bottom really think insurance is a symbol of loss of faith in God? If that had influenced his assessment of Downs, the strange story of trying to baptize his wife should have put an end to considering the man predictable. And now this phone call the very night of his acquittal made Howard Downs suddenly seem as complicated a person as Father Roger Dowling had ever known. As he lit his pipe, sending up great clouds of smoke, he felt a ghoulish excitement in anticipation of the visit. And he regretted that Phil was here.

It had been only fair to tell Downs the captain of detectives was in the rectory. He had feared the news would scare Downs off, but not at all, he professed to be happy about it. When the doorbell rang, Father Dowling got up. In the hallway he turned and saw Marie in the kitchen doorway looking forlorn.

"I'll get it, Marie."

"If you like."

"It's so late," he offered by way of ambiguous apology.

"Hmmph."

Howard Downs stood in the light of the porch lamp like someone just apprised that he was on Candid Camera. There was a faint smile on his face and he looked here and there as if in search of the camera. The priest hesitated a moment before opening the door. Downs had been dressed for the trial in the theatrical sense of the term. Neat, kempt, but no sign of prosperity. He had changed his clothes since afternoon and even Roger Dowling could see that the suit he wore was of the best. Much about him was different, but not the smoking. Downs seemed more intent than ever to do damage to his lungs and heart. At the sound of the doorknob turning, Downs's smile fled, and when Roger Dowling opened the door the insurance man wore an abject expression.

"It's good of you to see me at this ungodly hour, Father Dowling. But I have to talk to someone. Is Captain Keegan still here?"

"We can talk alone in the parlor if you'd like."

"Oh, he may as well hear it."

All emerged over the course of the next hour and a half, bringing the hands on the study clock close to three in the morning. Marie, yawning, pasty faced, her curiosity sufficiently assuaged, had gone back to bed after the first half hour, wisely; the main facts were out by that time.

This was Downs's incredible story. Although he was innocent of his wife's death — there was no wavering on that score — he had fully expected to be found guilty. For reasons he had gone into with Father Dowling, if not Captain Keegan, he was almost willing to accept punishment for a crime he had not committed. "A new experience," he said and tried to smile, unsuccessfully. He had seen Roger Dowling in the courtroom, right after the verdict, and had wanted to talk with him.

"My God, if only I had!" There was genuine emotion in Downs's voice.

■ 32 ■

Instead he had been surrounded by friends and foes and the curious and finally he and Farrell were hustled from the courtroom and back to the witness room for their own safety. Farrell had a bottle of Irish whiskey in his briefcase, claiming he had brought it in the full expectation of an acquittal and now by God they were going to celebrate. The judge was brought in, the prosecutor, the little room was soon more packed than the courtroom. Downs gave a vivid picture of the flamboyant Farrell filling paper cups with the precious liquid and then proposing a toast to himself.

"To himself?"

"To himself. He allowed as how there had been skeptics who thought an innocent man might suffer in this case, he had reason to think that even his client's faith in the happy outcome had dimmed along the way, but he wanted everyone to know that Vincent Arthur Farrell had never doubted. And then he added, 'Friends, I was certain I would get him off even if he had done it.' That got a big laugh, of course. I guess that was the beginning of a motive."

"Motive for what?" Phil Keegan was impatient with all this folderol, but then it wasn't his party. He had, ten minutes after Downs got started, telephoned Cy Horvath and given him very specific instructions.

"I mean, that is when I began to want to kill Farrell."

"Because he made a little joke?"

"Captain, it is not a little joke to me. And I saw it was not something that was going to pass over. For the rest of his life, Farrell would be braying about his great triumph and I would be treated in my own town like someone who had been spared punishment for a crime it was generally understood I had committed. I let the joke, as you call it, go, but that other thought began festering inside me. I had never liked Farrell. I despised him. I hated his flowing white hair, his silly bow ties, his silly checked suits and those rings. Did you ever notice the rings he wears? One on every finger almost. *The Lord of the Rings.* And now I was tied to that clown for the rest of my life."

"You've read Tolkien?" Roger Dowling asked.

Downs looked at him blankly.

"*The Lord of the Rings,*" the priest repeated.

"Yes. Farrell. Prison suddenly seemed preferable to being linked to that charlatan for the rest of my life."

"If it weren't for that charlatan, you would still be in jail."

"Captain, in a way, that is my point."

Cy Horvath called to say the body of Vincent Arthur Farrell, attorney at law, had been found in the parking lot behind the Casa Polenta, just as Downs said it would be.

"We ate there," Downs said.

"Just the two of you?"

"Father, it was not an occasion when Farrell was likely to want to be alone. There were eight or nine others, people I had never met and would never have met except for the circumstances."

"Why did you go?"

Downs smiled tolerantly at Keegan. "It would have seemed small to refuse the invitation. I should have invited him, by all rights, but I don't think even Farrell himself thought of that. It didn't matter. It would all show up on my bill anyway, or rather would not show up. I knew I was going to pay through the nose."

Keegan said, "So you went to dinner with him figuring you were paying for it anyway?"

"That is an afterthought, Captain Keegan. I went because it seemed impossible not to."

"How did Farrell die?" Father Dowling asked.

Keegan said, "There was a towel wrapped around his throat,

a very long roll towel from the machine in the men's room of the Casa Polenta. You let him eat before you killed him, is that it?"

Downs seemed to decide not to let this get to him. He took a deep breath and spoke calmly. "I did not sit down to table with him intending to kill him afterward. The idea grew in my mind as the meal progressed."

"Did you find out who the others were?"

"Father, I suppose they were sleazy lawyers like Farrell, courthouse hangers-about. After Farrell toasted himself they vied with one another to raise a glass in his honor. I suppose it was a way to keep the wine flowing."

"What were some of the names?" Keegan asked.

Downs dismissed the question with a flutter of fingers. "Introductions were made. If I caught any names I didn't remember them a minute later. I had been through a harrowing experience, Captain. Unjustly accused, yet willing to accept a verdict of guilty, I was suddenly pushed back into a world I had not expected to see again. In company I would not have chosen. Anyway, I am sure the waiters and the owner of the Casa Polenta can provide the names. The owner's name is Figlio. He looks like a crook."

"He has done time," Keegan said.

"Maybe all my dinner companions had. That would make them typical clients of Farrell, I imagine."

Keegan leaned toward Downs. "I am asking you now as a policeman, formally, and I am a damned fool for not doing this at once. You don't have to tell me anything without having a lawyer present."

"A lawyer! No thanks."

"Are you confessing to the murder of Vincent Arthur Farrell?"

Downs nodded.

"I want a vocal answer."

■ 35 ■

"Very well. I confess vocally to the murder of my erstwhile lawyer, Vincent Arthur Farrell."

"You're under arrest."

"It's nice to be home. Did I mention how attractive prison seemed when I was with that gang at the Casa Polenta? Even more attractive than when I was sure it was only a matter of time until I was doing some."

Was this the standard repartee of an insurance man? Roger Dowling could not remember if Downs had spoken in this snippy, almost fey way, when they had their conferences in the county jail. Then Downs had seemed a beaten man, resigned to his fate, even though it was one he insisted he did not deserve. Now, by his own account, he was guilty of murder, and here he sat jaunty as could be, puffing cigarettes, fencing with Keegan, apparently without a worry in the world. Nor did his story make a great deal of sense. The fear that he would from now on be known as the man who had killed his wife with impunity did not seem to lead logically to the desire to kill the lawyer who had won his freedom. Indeed, now he seemed intent on making sure that the world, via the pastor of St. Hilary's, knew of his heinous deed. And of course the possibility of being the constant object of whispered gossip need not be realized. He had only to move. He was wealthy. His agency could continue to earn money for him even in his absence. He had no ties in Fox River.

It was another thing that struck Roger about both the Downses. She and he had both been born in Fox River; they had lived here all their lives, yet each was all the other had in the world. There were no children. There were no brothers and sisters. Mrs. Downs's mother was still alive, ninety-seven years old, senile in a nursing home.

"Well," Keegan said. "We better go downtown."

"Howard," Father Dowling said, rising, "this time I think you had better choose a lawyer."

■ 36 ■

"To get me off? For that I need a shyster."

"Tuttle's probably too busy to take your case," Keegan said, and he could not repress a smile.

The three of them were standing now. Downs was the tallest and neither Captain Keegan nor Father Dowling were short men. Downs said, "I will hire the best criminal lawyer in Fox River, thus assuring that justice will be done."

They moved down the hall to the front door, three men breaking up late after a long and fascinating conversation.

5

TUTTLE HAD fallen asleep in his office, feet on the desk, hat pulled low over his eyes. Peanuts Pianone snored away on the couch. They had topped off a night of commiseration with a liter of California burgundy. Neither man was awaited anywhere by anyone so it had seemed sensible enough to fall asleep where they were.

Tuttle wakened once, an hour or two after having fallen asleep, and knew he would regret it in the morning for having snoozed like this. He was no longer able to work for days on end with little or no rest, catching a nap here or there, and feeling no worse for wear when it was all over. Work. The word was as nostalgic as youth. He had lied when he suggested he had been approached to act as attorney for Howard Downs. Fat chance. But then, it had been almost as fat a chance that Farrell would end up with a client like him. Just for fun, if you could call it fun, he had checked out Downs. The guy was loaded. He had to be. In fact, the more Tuttle looked into Downs and the Downs Agency the more incredible it seemed that he had actually been brought up on a murder rap. Tuttle could almost believe Downs when he pleaded innocent. What the hell need did he have to kill his wife? He wasn't Catholic. He could divorce her, pay her off, live happily ever after. But the fact was, Downs was caught between two women, his wife and Phyllis Whitmore. Yet this only made it odder that he had permitted events to get away from him.

Tuttle achieved such self-understanding as he had by imagining that successful people had a knack for getting a hand on events. He wasn't too sure what that meant. But then, if he had been, he would have had the knack. On the Downs case, he laid it all out for Peanuts, speaking with great authority and without a single warble of doubt in his voice. This was because it was doubtful Peanuts understood a word he said.

Pianone was an officer in the Fox River police force thanks to family connections. Both his father and brother were members of the city council, and the Pianones, who had lived on the shady side of the law in past times, were now on the other side of the legal tracks, making laws as well as breaking them. It would not be fair to say of Peanuts that he was retarded. It would certainly not be wise to voice such an opinion within the hearing of any member of the Pianone family. The prospect of being washed up on the banks of the Fox River or simply feeding the fish at its bottom would then become a distinct possibility. Peanuts did have a high school diploma, though what coercion had gone into the awarding of it Tuttle did not know. He did know that Peanuts could read. He was an avid student of comic books, poring over them with the devotion of a rabbi studying the Torah.

Tuttle considered Peanuts a friend, which, translated, meant that Peanuts proved valuable to him from time to time, letting him in on inside dope from headquarters, knowledge of which Peanuts was as likely to have from sitting at his father's or brother's table as from his colleagues on the force. In turn, Tuttle befriended Peanuts, taking him to dinner at least once every two weeks, Chinese as often as not. Peanuts loved Chinese and Tuttle himself would have betrayed his country for a plate of chicken fried rice. Perhaps as important an element as any in their relation was that Tuttle could feel indisputably Peanuts's intellectual superior and speak to him as he could to no one else. Thus it had been to Peanuts that he had elaborated his understanding of the case of Howard Downs.

"He is caught in a horny dilemma. Not only can he be divorced by his wife and get hit for big money, the Whitmore dame can stick him for palimony. You know what palimony is? That means if you been keeping some broad for years she acquires some of the rights of a regular spouse. Like the right to bleed you white if you decide to dump her. Whitmore knows about the wife. The question is, does the wife know about Whitmore? If she didn't, she was a bigger idiot than her husband. Half the town knew about Downs and Phyllis Whitmore."

Tuttle meant that it had not taken him long to learn of the liaison. The first clue had come when Peanuts was engaged in one of his racist tirades against Agnes Lamb, the black cop he refused to work with. Peanuts might have an IQ below a hundred but he knew which was the master race.

"A wife has got to suspect when her husband is running around."

Where Tuttle had gained this certainty it would be hard to say. Perhaps from listening to the gabble of other lawyers. Since he had never married, he had no personal basis for the claim. But granting its truth and the wit to hire such a lawyer as himself, the facts would have come out in short order and she would have been free from the perfidious Downs, with a good deal of his past and future income secured to her account. Oh, if only she had come to him in time.

"Why couldn't he just leave well enough alone?" Peanuts asked. It was moments like this that made Tuttle think Peanuts was not all that many cards short of a full deck.

"Right. Exactly. As far as he is concerned, the situation is what it is. So he leaves it alone. His only fear is that one or the other woman is going to stick him for some cash. So what? There is a lot more where that came from. Besides, who pays their full alimony anymore?"

That quickly Tuttle changed sides. If Downs, sued by his wife for divorce, had come to him, they would have worked out a no-fault settlement that would have made the other attorney's head spin. The first move would be to conceal the extent of Downs's income....

It was such easeful thoughts as this that brought Tuttle sleep a second time in his office that night. He dreamed, and in his dream Downs had actually consulted another lawyer. Not just another lawyer, someone Tuttle knew. The odious face was forming in his dreaming mind when the phone snapped him awake.

The shrill ringing in the diminutive office seemed incredibly loud. It sounded like an alarm rather than a signal. Peanuts sat up like a Swiss Army knife, got his feet on the floor, and walked rapidly into the opposite wall. Obviously he did not know where he was. Tuttle grabbed the phone before it could make more racket.

"Tuttle and Tuttle." One-eyed, he made out the time on his watch. Five-thirty. It felt like one or two.

"Where's Giovanni?"

The voice immediately filled Tuttle with terrified fear. Peanuts's father! It was Tuttle's practice straightaway to scrub from his mind any and every story he heard about the Pianones like an adolescent getting rid of bad thoughts. He did not want to know anything about Peanuts's family.

"We had dinner together last night."

"He didn't go home."

"Neither did I."

"Where is he?"

Peanuts had come to a standstill in front of Tuttle's desk. "Gimme the key to the john."

"It's your father," Tuttle said, muffling the phone.

Peanuts's mouth fell open. He was scared but he wasn't crazy. He took the phone.

"Hello, Papa."

Tuttle watched Peanuts's face as he talked with his father. Or listened. He began to nod. Fear left his face. He hung up.

"Farrell's been killed."

"What!" But immediately Tuttle checked his reaction. Was he being let in on a little family secret?

"My father doesn't like it. He wants you to look into it. He's mad as hell. It happened behind my cousin's restaurant."

"Your father's hiring me?"

Peanuts thought about that. "He wants you to find out who killed Farrell."

6

THERE ARE men who drink in secret, there are men who cheat on their wives, there are those who gross out on junk food from time to time. Lieutenant Cyril Horvath of the Fox River police was a secret jogger.

He was a huge, barrel-chested man, with close-cropped nondescript hair and a broad expressionless face that bore signs of the ravages of teen-age acne. But in his teens it had been his athletic prowess rather than his complexion for which he had been known. He was varsity in three sports, hockey, football, and baseball. He played defense in hockey and football, a member of the Mike Ditka school, where might makes fright. In baseball he played first base and could kiss a ball a mile into a brisk wind. It was understood that he would play college sports and, who knows, maybe go on to a professional career. This was not a solitary dream. His coaches talked openly about it. In his senior year he received scholarship offers from four places, none of them first rate. Cargo Linda, a California junior college, had been the most attractive, since it was a feeder for Southern Cal. His future looked clear. But he was never to go to college; his career in sports ended when he graduated from high school.

What all the confident predictors, what the representatives of the minor colleges who approached him could not know, was that a cancer had been growing in the body of Horvath's father for more than a year. He had felt discomfort, he had felt pain, but a man who has worked at the controls of a Caterpillar earth mover no longer thinks of himself as fragile. By the time he was forced to acknowledge the pain was unbearable there was nothing that could be done for him. Perhaps there never had been and he was smart to go on as long as he could. Horvath's mother wanted Cyril to go to college, play sports, become famous, by which she meant, stay famous. In their neighborhood everyone knew Cy. Somehow she would manage to put food on the table for herself and the little Horvaths — and all his brothers and sisters were younger than Cy. He told her once and once was enough that he would get a job and keep some money coming in. He turned his back on an attractive future, took a job with the Fox River street department as a tree trimmer, and prepared himself to take the exam for the police department. His size would be an advantage as a cop. If he regretted what might have been, he never said so to anyone. Not to his mother, not to his brothers and sisters, not later to his wife. He bore whatever pain there was the way his father had borne the cancer. But in his case, the pain diminished rather than increased. He knew the intensity of competition in professional athletics and how slim a chance he would have had. For that matter, he had no guarantee he would make it big at even a small college. There are many thoughts that cushion the blow of disappointment.

One thing Cy never lost was the habit of keeping himself in shape. As a lineman he had eaten to put on weight and he knew what could happen to him once he stopped exercising. But he did not want to be a failed jock, hanging around gyms, pumping iron, working up a sweat. Mr. America? Forget it. Cy would not want to be alone in an elevator with any of the body-beautiful guys. He ran. He jogged. The popularity of this exercise made involvement in it safe from comment. Everybody jogged. Jiggling women and straining men filled the paths in the parks and the walks along the Fox River while fleet young people flew past them with Walkmans shutting them off from the world. It got to be crowded. Cy shared the comments Keegan made about the craze. When Chief Robertson actually showed up in his office one day in a sweat suit and tennies, the bottom had been reached. The chief's outfit was to a real sweat suit what a tuxedo is to a set of dungarees. It looked tailored. From that day on jogging was a dirty word in the Fox River Police Department, and it did not matter that Robertson's interest in the exercise flagged the second day and was gone after the third. "Going jogging" became a euphemism for crossing the street to the Florida for a drink.

All of these factors made Horvath a secret jogger. Each morning he rose between six-thirty and seven. By five minutes after the hour he was running. Fifteen minutes out, fifteen minutes back, steady routine was better than a grueling excess. This morning he eased himself out the back door and started down the drive to the street at 6:45. It had been twenty-nine hours since they had found the body of Vinny Farrell behind the Casa Polenta, and Horvath looked forward to the monotony of running to help put some order into the events.

He had been asleep when Keegan called from Father Dowling's and told him to check out, on the QT, a rumor that there was a body behind the Casa Polenta.

"Anyone I know?"

"Vincent Arthur Farrell."

Cy waited but there was no chuckle, no alteration of the sound of Keegan's breathing to indicate that the captain was pulling his leg. "How'd you hear?"

"If he's there, I'll tell you. I'll tell you if he isn't there. Later. For now, as a favor, go take a look, will you, Cy?"

Cy went. There wasn't much he wouldn't do for Phil Keegan. Keegan had taken the trouble to find out there was a mind in Cy's hulk of a body. He had noticed when Cy did something particularly well. He had moved him right along and then tapped him as his right-hand man in the detective division.

The work was largely routine. What the hell, life is largely routine. Cy Horvath was not looking for amusement from the universe. But it was work that required care and skill. And compassion. Whatever it was, his face, his manner, his size, he had an easy time interviewing people. At first he had feared it had everything to do with his size, that he intimidated people. Maybe they expected to get worked over if they didn't speak. But that wasn't it. He was just one of those people other people willingly told their troubles to. And trouble was the name of the game for a cop. Keegan came to rely on the knack Cy had of getting information where everyone else drew a blank. That alone could have explained his asking for a preliminary look into things at the Casa Polenta by Lieutenant Cyril Horvath.

Keegan called at two. By two-twenty Cy was pulling up in front of the restaurant. The owner, Gino Figlio, was related in some way to the Pianones, another reason Keegan might want to proceed with prudence. The restaurant was on a side street in downtown Fox River, its exterior still bathed in lights that had been mounted on municipal lamp posts. Maybe the city footed the bill. The object of this electric attention was a building that was chalk white, thanks to tons of stucco. It had red highlights due to bricks that did not seem quite real. They trimmed the corners of the building and formed a sort of grotto effect around the front entrance. A miniature fountain to the right of the entrance was shut down for the night, maybe the season. A canopy stretched to the curb, and a strip of indoor/outdoor carpeting led the arriving patrons to the door. There was a doorman, of course. A thug, supposedly reformed, named or called Sam Quintin. At two-twenty, Sam was smoking a cigar so big it looked like a comic's prop and he seemed at peace with the world. Until he saw Cy.

"What do you want, Horvath?"

Cy looked at his watch, prompting Sam to say they had a late license, so forget it. Cy had no intention of chatting with Sam. He pulled open the door himself and went inside, into the music, the voices, the smoke, the smell of food. Coming from his own bed he could not help thinking how joyless supposed pleasure is. Yet some people thought it fun to sit around in places like this until the wee hours of the morning.

Inside seemed like the night sky, with intermittent lights: the bar, the piano, candles like vigil lights on the tables. The piano player seemed to have his hair piece on backward and he was groaning into the microphone, making up in decibels what he lacked in voice.

"You the cop?"

Horvath turned but there was nobody there, at least at eye level. The voice came from a man three-quarters Horvath's height but his shoulders were broad enough for a man much taller. He was vaguely reminiscent of Peanuts, in size. Horvath could not make out the face.

"You Figlio?"

"Follow me."

They went through a curtain of strung beads into a hallway that was dimly but ordinarily lit. There was a camera mounted high in a corner at the end of the hallway and it moved slightly as Horvath and his guide drew nearer to the door. The camera must have been operated from inside the office. A buzzer sounded as they approached the door and the little man pushed right through.

"Wait here," he said, but a voice from within countermanded him.

"Come right in, Lieutenant Horvath."

The man behind the desk was standing, but he was no taller than the man who had guided Horvath here. "You can leave us alone, Mario."

"You're Gino Figlio?"

"Now, Lieutenant, you didn't come to the wrong address, did you? What are you doing up so late?"

"Early. I got a phone call. It woke me up. About this place."

"A call? I thought maybe you saw my ad."

"Did Mr. Farrell the lawyer have dinner here tonight?"

"Sit down, Horvath."

"How do you know who I am?"

"You're famous. How do you know who I am? Get the point? It's the same thing."

Cy did not get the point but he let it go.

"Sure, Farrell was here. A big celebration of his victory in court. I told him, you act this happy, people will think it don't happen too often." Figlio had collapsed into, rather than sat in, his chair, a plush item with cushions of rumpled leather and stainless steel frame. Obviously he was a man who appreciated his own jokes.

"When did he leave?"

"Who said he left?"

"He's still here?"

"Didn't you look around?"

"In the dining rooms? My eyes never got used to the dark. You got cameras out there too?"

Another laugh. "I got eyes out there, Horvath, but no cameras. You're right. There's not that much light. Maybe someday they'll make a camera I can afford that can be used out there. Want to see my system?"

Why not? If Farrell were alive and kicking in the dining room, he had come on a wild goose chase. If, on the other hand, he were lying dead behind the restaurant, a minute or two spent gaining Figlio's cooperation wasn't wasted.

There was an electric eye at the end of the hallway that, when tripped, automatically switched the channel on the set in the corner. Figlio changed channels now by punching a button on a panel on his desk. He had the sort of joystick Horvath had seen on video games to adjust and direct the camera.

"Very ingenious."

"Also, it records."

"Would you check your other system and see if Farrell's out there?"

"Sure." To Horvath's surprise, Figlio did this with a walkie-talkie. A punched button, a delay, and then, "Did Mr. Farrell go without saying good-by to me?" The question was accompanied with a chuckle and a smile. The smile disappeared as the crackled response told him Farrell wasn't there.

"When the hell did he leave?"

This system did not work as well as the television camera and finally, impatiently, Figlio ordered his minion to come in. Nothing after that was pleasing to the owner of the Casa Polenta. Horvath was willing to take Figlio's employee's word that Farrell was not in the dining room.

"Let's look out back, Figlio."

He had smelled the kitchen when they came through the beaded curtain and he guessed a left turn took you there. He headed that way and Figlio came with him, puffing, mad, but as curious as Horvath.

"What did you mean, you got a call?"

"Someone said Farrell is lying dead out back."

"Jesus, are you serious?"

"Let's see."

Figlio was lucky Keegan wasn't here. The captain could take bad language from people who didn't know any better, but Figlio had been taught the Commandments. Cy was not in the converting business, not that he thought Figlio was a likely customer.

They were winding down in the kitchen, cleaning up, doing some preparations for the following day, or just sitting around.

The look on Figlio's face brought the cooks and waiters to their feet, but Cy just kept going toward the door. Outside, with the door shut, it was quiet, the air was impossibly fresh, and a single light cast a feeble glow into an area enclosed by concrete block walls at least fifteen feet high. The back corners were in shadow and it was in one of them they found the body.

Cy crouched next to the body, verified that it was Farrell, and that he was likely dead. "How many ways into this area?"

"You just came through it."

"What's beyond the walls?"

"Other people's property."

"No alley?"

"There's no way to it."

"What's the point of the yard?"

"There is no point. I may expand the kitchen this way."

Back in the kitchen, Horvath lined up everyone there. They seemed a scruffy group to be entrusted with the preparation of food, but how many restaurant kitchens had he seen?

"How many people went through that door tonight?"

He had expected confused and conflicting answers, but not what he got. Unanimously, they denied that anyone had gone through the back door outside.

"Oh, come on. Mr. Figlio and I just went through it. That's two."

The chef smiled crookedly as if Horvath had just won a game of chance. "Okay. You two. But nobody else."

That was when Horvath called Keegan to tell him the bad news was true. Farrell was dead, apparently strangled.

"You alone, Cy?"

"That's what you wanted."

"I'll call downtown and get things moving. I'll be there myself as soon as I can."

"You got a list of the people who ate here tonight?" he asked Figlio after he hung up.

"All the reservations, sure."

"There were people who didn't have reservations, though?"

Figlio said yes, but no strangers, if that's what Horvath was after.

"Okay, let's lock the front door."

"You want me to close?"

"I don't want anyone leaving here."

Figlio protested, of course, but then the crew from the medical examiner's office arrived on the heels of two squad cars and not even the bellowing tenor in the main dining room could drown out the excitement. By now it was a lot closer to morning than to the night before. Agnes Lamb came at four-thirty and Cy put her in charge of questioning the patrons.

"What do we want to know, mainly?" Agnes always looked right at you with her large liquid eyes when she talked to you. Cy liked that.

"Did they notice anything? Were they aware of the Farrell party? Did they see when he left?"

"Do we know who was with him?"

"We may know who killed him. This is largely routine."

"Who did it?"

"Downs."

Her brows went up, her eyes widened, and her lips puckered in surprise. "You're kidding!" Immediately she put a hand on his arm. "No. I'm kidding. Of course you mean it. How do we know?"

"He confessed."

"Well, let's hope this time he doesn't receive absolution."

7

MICHELLE MORAN, at twenty-seven, was right on schedule, or so
at least she thought herself to be much of the time. In college she
had resolved to become a New Woman, ambitious, efficient, bent
on success. Originally she had planned to add an MBA to her un-
dergraduate major in economics, but when she saw that MBAs
were a drug on the market she decided to go right to work after
she graduated. Her head was full of grandiose plans when she sat
down to talk about them with Mr. Downs.

   Mr. Downs had sold her father the policy that had permitted
her to go to the school of her choice, and that meant Northwestern.
After her father died and the wisdom of having the coverage became clear, Mr. Downs continued to advise Mrs. Moran, and
what had been no modest amount to begin with became over the
years a sizable nest egg. It had permitted Michelle's mother to
move to Orlando when she turned fifty — "Go ahead, tell people,
I don't care. I wish you would. They'll think I'm a lot older, retir-
ing to Florida" — ending one of Michelle's more pleasant day-
dreams. Mr. Downs had been so good to them that Michelle wondered if there wasn't something more. Could he be half in love
with her mother? Incredible as that at first seemed, it became a
familiar thought, and Michelle would imagine the two of them
emerging from one of their sessions with the big announcement.
But the only change was that she was asked to sit in on the discussions. She was already doing this in high school. It seemed the

most natural thing in the world to discuss her educational plans with Mr. Downs as well.

She had several uncles, but they were laborers who would know nothing of money and who would probably resent it if they knew how well fixed her mother was. Since Mr. Downs had been the architect of their security, there were no secrets from him. He approved of her decision not to waste two more years getting an MBA.

She said, "If I get one, it will be at a company's expense. The First National Bank does that, so do lots of other firms."

"That's not my policy."

She did not understand what he meant.

"I'm offering you a job, Michelle. In my agency."

"Insurance?"

"What do you know about insurance?" She thought she knew a lot, but it certainly didn't take her long to tell it. Mr. Downs smiled.

"What do you think a person like myself, with an independent agency, earns a year?"

Like a moron, she guessed. She was laughably low. She couldn't believe it.

"Michelle, you will be more independent sooner and a lot richer coming in with me than if you take a job on the bottom rung of the biggest and best corporation in Chicago."

She didn't say yes right away. Somehow it was a bit disappointing to think she had spent all that time in school and dreamed all those dreams only to settle down in Fox River, Illinois. Local girl makes good, but who would care?

"What do you want, applause or success?"

"Can't I have both?"

For answer, Mr. Downs clapped his hands slowly, looking right at her. It seemed the nicest possible thing he could have done, and it was all she could do not to cry. It made her all the sadder that nothing had come of her mother and Howard Downs.

Mrs. Downs was an impediment Michelle had not known about when she first dreamed her girlish daydream. After she went to work for Mr. Downs — "Call me Howie, for God's sake" — she came to see that Mrs. Downs was an impediment only because Howie was loyal. He had married her, he was stuck with her, and that was that. At least, that is what she had thought at first.

When she learned about Howard and Phyllis Whitmore, Michelle went into a deep depression. She felt as she would have felt on learning her own father was unfaithful. Because Howie had become her father, in a way. There was something else too. She had done well at school, she was doing well at the Downs Agency, there was little doubt in her own or others' minds that she would be a very successful businesswoman. Howie had not exaggerated the possibilities for wealth on the part of the independent agent and already Michelle dreamed of eventually starting her own agency. With all doubt seemingly removed from her business success, she had a hollow feeling that being successful was not the point of life. There was also love.

She had always been popular, she had her circle of friends, but she was equally close to them all. Many people liked her, but did anybody love her? Did she love anybody? It seemed terrible that she could not answer yes.

She did not mean love with a small l. The only love that interested her was one that would absorb her totally. She realized that her notion of combining marriage and a career presupposed that no one thing was supremely important to her. But she could not vacillate between two kinds of life. For all her success, she now knew her career could never claim her totally. It was shortly after this realization that she learned of Howie and Phyllis Whitmore.

Phyllis Whitmore! The woman was more difficult to believe

than that Howie really was cheating on his wife. Phyllis was everything that was wrong with women in business, at least women of a certain age. Phyllis still did not believe in her heart of hearts that she belonged. She acted like an intruder. She was always proving herself. Worse, she was always imagining sexist attitudes in the associates of the agency. This seemed to come down to the fact that they did not take her as seriously as she took herself. Besides, they knew about her affair with Howie and doubtless inferred—who could blame them—that her promotion to office manager and then associate had been won horizontally rather than vertically.

That was the quaint way Gene Lane, the youngest associate, had put it. He actually had that sign on his door: Eugene Lane— The Youngest Associate.

"I'm surprised Phyl doesn't make you take it down."

"Now, now. It's sexist to think women are more edgy about their age than men."

Gene was, on the surface, the least serious person she knew. He never gave a straight answer when a facetious one would do. He was about her height; his mustache was more idea than reality; his sandy hair was wispy and thin ("Who wants fat hair?"); he was pudgy and his torso was too long or his legs too short. He was thirty-one and single and said he cried himself to sleep every night and Michelle knew he wasn't really kidding. That was the danger with men like Gene. They engaged her sympathy and there was no easy way to stop them from joking her into something serious. It was Gene who told her about Howie and Phyllis.

"I don't believe it."

"What's to believe? It's a fact. Everyone knows it."

"Well, *I* don't know it."

"You're someone, all right. Well, you know now."

"I had my eye on him myself." And she dug Gene in the ribs. He affected her like that.

■ 55 ■

It was true. Once she knew, she knew. Given the character of Mrs. Downs, it was hard to blame Howie. But Phyllis Whitmore!

Why couldn't he choose someone nice, someone who wouldn't take advantage? Phyllis had to know that everyone else in the office knew and she seemed to dare them to make the slightest allusion to it. Why couldn't he have chosen someone like...

Like me.

The shocking thought did not shock for long, but it did frighten her. Mr. Downs? He was old enough to be her father. He was her father, in a way. The thought was incestuous.

The Friday morning Gene came and told her that Mr. Downs was back in jail, this time for the murder of his lawyer, Farrell, Michelle knew better than to think he was kidding. Why are some things so incredible they're credible? Not that she thought for a moment that Howie was any more guilty this time than he had been last time. Last time! The nightmare was hardly over and it had begun again. That wasn't fair. It was silly and stupid and made no sense, but her first reaction was to blame Phyllis Whitmore. It was not woman's intuition. It was not a rational deduction. The conviction rose spontaneously from her darker desires. She wanted it to be Phyllis. All the while she listened to the few details Gene had, Michelle was saying to herself: She did it. Phyl is responsible. And this time she is going to pay.

8

THE ATMOSPHERE in the press room was different from any Mervel had ever experienced. The handful of jaded, skeptical and morose upholders of the public's right to know were clearly stunned by the news that Downs had confessed to the murder of Vincent Arthur Farrell.

"Was Farrell murdered?"

"Have charges been brought?"

"Did he sign a confession?"

The right questions, the routine questions, were all asked, and answers received, but Mervel knew he wasn't alone in thinking they were going through some charade. Downs had made a mockery of the news they had all enthused over in the stories the previous day. Local Businessman Acquitted of Wife Slaying. Mervel had used the word uxoricide, but of course Hopkins had cut it. And rightly so. He hadn't needed the word to bring out the pathos of what had happened. Implicit in his account was that Downs was guilty but that he had triumphed over the law. Rich boy makes good. System screwed by insurance man. In being acquitted, Downs had become crazily enough the little guy who wins against enormous odds, the underdog. Underdog! But mentioning Downs's wealth only added zest to the story. Here was someone who could afford to enjoy the freedom his lawyer had won for him. Farrell had been more difficult to dramatize, he did the job too well himself.

Now, twenty-four hours later, Downs was back in jail and the whole thing would begin again. It was enough to make you give up on the news. That, and the grating presence of the pretty people from television, who as usual took over the session. Wayne Hanson, Robertson's new press secretary, wanted to keep it short and sweet, but he was willing to do anything to get more time on the tube.

"What was the motive?"

"We're not yet in a position to answer that question." Hanson, a strawberry blond with slightly exophthalmic blue eyes, got into position to have his best side caught by the handheld camera. The hand that held it was Swannie's, who once had earned an honest living at the *Messenger* and now in jeans and tennis shoes and a tee shirt with the legend Curse My Ash emblazoned over the international no smoking symbol scurried around like a schoolboy.

"Where did the murder occur?"

"The body was found behind a local restaurant. The Casa Polenta. I'll spell that." And he did. You would have thought he was taking part in the final round of a spelling bee. He pronounced the letters with exaggerated distinction while Swannie, genuflecting before him, caught it all on film. Figlio was not going to appreciate that ad.

It was painful, but Mervel stayed until it was over. Swannie swooped at him with his camera on the way out but Mervel didn't even duck. He knew it wasn't on.

"Go to hell, Swannie."

"I have. It's called television." The cameraman's eyes were bloodshot and his frizzed hair made him look like one of the Three Stooges.

"Got time for a drink?"

"You're on." He pronounced it urine, but his meaning was clear.

Swannie stashed his gear in his car and they went to the Florida across the street. It was ten in the morning. Swannie had a glass of beer and a shot of blended whiskey. "I'm cutting down," he explained. "Did I tell you about the Foreign Legion?"

"They accepted you."

"In their mess is a sign: 'Alcohol kills.' Underneath: 'A Legionnaire does not fear death.' Then: 'Alcohol kills slowly.' Finally: 'A Legionnaire is in no hurry.' " Swannie punched Mervel painfully on the arm.

"What do you make of the Farrell thing?"

Swannie had to think. Behind his camera, he lived in a special world. How many news events had he covered without noticing what the hell was going on? "The guy has acquired a bad habit. He keeps this up, he'll bring back the death penalty."

"It is back."

"No kidding. I'll behave."

Someone shoved against Mervel, pushing him farther into the booth. Tuttle. He looked like hell. Mervel told him so.

"Sticks and stones. What kind of juice are we having this morning?"

"Potato. Did you hear about Farrell?"

Tuttle smirked. Mervel realized that, ravaged as the lawyer looked, he was neat as a pin. Clean shirt, a good suit, shaved. And he wasn't wearing that goddamn tweed hat. "I was put into the picture early," Tuttle said.

"You do look like hell," Swannie said.

Tuttle ignored him. "How did Hanson do?"

"He photographs well. Not that he will get on the air. Maybe a fraction of a second. Or his voice in voice-over." Swannie smiled malevolently. It was his opportunity to distort events by editing the film on which the ineffable Bruce commented. Mervel liked being a reporter, but he didn't like the thought of such power in the hands of people like Swannie and Bruce.

"I knew you when you were good," Tuttle said. "Downs didn't do it."

"Can I quote you on that?"

"Just remember you heard it here first."

9

FATHER DOWLING did not go to the county jail until two the following afternoon. He said his regular Mass at noon, the Saturday Mass; at five-thirty he would say a Mass anticipating the Sunday obligation. There was not much demand for this afternoon Mass in St. Hilary, most of whose members found the old ways best and accepted such changes as Father Dowling introduced with neither enthusiasm nor rebellion. Saying Mass at noon each weekday seemed the best solution, though several women, Marie Murkin among them, missed the punishing habit of rising in the dark and attending Mass at six. Great admirer of tradition as he was, Father Dowling could not say he missed it. He had never felt quite awake until he had had his breakfast. The solution would have been to retire earlier, but he derived such consolation from sitting up late, reading in his study, that he seldom got to bed before two. Now at least he could enjoy six hours' sleep.

It was going on two when he was admitted into the cell block where Howard Downs was being held. The concrete floor, the aspect of steel and mesh and confinement, affected the priest strongly and he wondered how men could remain cooped up like this without losing their minds. Downs, clad in the freshly washed dungarees of a prisoner, sat on his bunk, back against the wall, reading. And smoking. But then, everyone smoked here. It seemed to add to the scofflaw atmosphere.

Downs looked up from his book as if he had not been expecting Roger Dowling.

"I brought you more books."

"Not mysteries, I hope. I hate mysteries."

"Have you ever read C. S. Lewis?"

"*Main Street*?"

"No, no. The friend of Tolkien's. He wrote a trilogy I have always liked. It doesn't seem quite right to call it science fiction."

The guard opened the cell door during this exchange and Father Dowling went inside. Downs moved to the toilet, giving his guest the bed to sit on.

"I asked for the same cell as before, but it's occupied."

"How long were you free?"

"Free?" Downs repeated the word as if he found its sound strange. He looked around his cell. "This really isn't all that bad."

"For a visit. How old are you, Howard?"

"Fifty-three. I know what you're thinking. A prison sentence, even a light one, and I would come out an old man."

"Yes. On the other hand, you could be acquitted again."

"This time I'm guilty."

"That does not prevent an acquittal."

"I doubt that I can count on that."

"Tell me about yourself. We have talked, how many times, nine, ten, maybe more, and I don't feel I know you at all. You're a native of Fox River, I know that much. Tell me about your growing up, your family, going to school."

"You're beginning to sound like the psychologist I had to talk to last time."

"God forbid. But the past is prologue."

"I suppose it is."

And Downs began to talk, hesitatingly at first, then with increasing ease. Who is uninterested in the subject of himself? Had Downs never before seen his life as a story, a drama? But for all of

Downs's sudden volubility, the account he gave of his life was remarkably superficial, as if his mind had been wholly absorbed in the exterior world. He was an only child, as was his wife. There was only her mother. They had been married nineteen, almost twenty years when Gloria was killed. School. He had attended John Calhoun, Fox River Central, and the University of Southern Illinois. His agency had been his life since there were no children.

"That's too bad."

"We didn't think so. Gloria and I were essentially selfish. We had no desire to become the unpaid servants of children. I have seen how parents worry about their offspring."

"As husbands about their wives, and vice versa."

"There is a great deal of difference in a mutual self-interest pact and the wide-open claims kids make on their parents."

"Yours does not sound like a very romantic marriage."

"There aren't any, Father Dowling. Marriages are generally unhappy. The trade-offs never give a perfect balance. Gloria used me and I used her. By and large, it was satisfactory."

"Surely it didn't start out like that."

"Oh, no. Like everybody else, we dreamed of constant violins and moonlight. When you see that marriage is anything but that, a crucial choice must be made. Many people, I think it is approximately fifty percent, divorce. The rest enter into a more or less conscious truce."

"Did your wife know about Phyllis Whitmore?"

"About her? She knew that my relationship with Phyl was more than a business one."

"And she didn't care?"

"We never discussed it."

"Then how do you know she knew?"

He smiled. "I knew. There is male intuition too. You must find all this shocking."

It would not do to tell Downs what he really thought of it,

but he was unlikely to be shocked by yet another story of human weakness. Did Downs imagine that he found his infidelity some extraordinary feat of sophistication?

"You had a truce with Phyllis Whitmore too?"

"In effect. But part of such arrangements is that one doesn't call a spade a spade. Women have a great appetite for self-deception."

"I suppose we all do."

Downs nodded, but his expression suggested that he at least had looked on himself with a cold eye and both knew and accepted exactly what he was. None of this fitted in with his confession to the murder of Vincent Arthur Farrell. Roger Dowling said this.

"Where could I run to?"

Phil Keegan had come to the noon Mass at St. Hilary and afterward had told Roger Dowling some of the results of the investigation at the Casa Polenta.

"Roger, we don't get much help at a place like that. They would have denied Farrell's victory dinner took place there if they could. Downs? Nobody admits having seen him. Nobody who works at the restaurant, that is. But Phyllis Whitmore was there too."

"Is that right?"

Howard Downs looked thoughtful when Roger told him the employees at the Casa Polenta did not corroborate his story of having had dinner with Farrell.

"They will. Not being cooperative with a police investigation is probably second nature to Figlio and the people who work for him. When they see that telling the truth can't hurt them, they will. They can't deny the body."

"It was where you said."

Downs nodded.

"The police and everyone else still assume that you killed your wife as well as Farrell."

"I know."

"Who did kill her?"

"I don't think anyone else has seriously asked me that question. Father, I don't know. I wish I could say there were valuables missing, things I wouldn't want the IRS to know about. But it wasn't a robbery. There was no sexual assault. It was just a brutal pointless slaying."

"Do you think your wife had any truces with other men?"

He smiled away the question. "Not likely."

"Why?"

Downs looked at him speculatively. "I'm always afraid I'm going to shock you. Put it this way. Gloria had tried sex and did not find it overwhelmingly attractive."

"There is more to life than sex. More to friendships."

"I don't think Gloria had any friends. She had been very close to her mother, but after we put the old girl in the nursing home, they became slightly estranged."

"You visited her regularly?"

"Gloria was pretty good about that."

"Her murderer should be found."

"Tell it to the police."

"They consider the case solved. You might launch your own investigation."

Downs frowned. "What do you mean?"

"Hire a detective."

"A private detective? What could he discover that the police haven't?"

"I don't think it's unfair to say the police investigation was not vigorous. They thought they had the murderer. You. They were seeking more conclusive evidence that you had done it. But they already believed they had sufficient proof. Now, if you hired someone who would begin with the assumption you had not killed her, well, something might turn up..."

"I'll think about it."

"It would be expensive, I suppose."

"That isn't a problem."

"Think about it."

Downs considered the burning tip of his cigarette. "No, money isn't the problem."

"What is?"

"It's hard to wish this on anyone," Downs said, looking around the cell.

Even the man who murdered his wife? Even a wife he had not loved? If Downs's life was really governed by self-interest alone, his magnanimity was not to be believed. Least of all could he be believed when he said he had murdered Vincent Arthur Farrell and wanted to pay the price.

10

SALLY WISE had been in nursing long enough to see what had once been a noble calling deteriorate. In hospitals there were so many grades and species of people who were not RNs dealing with the sick that it honestly made you wonder why more tragedies did not happen. Candy-stripers and Gray Ladies were one thing; so too volunteers who, although they got in the way, knew they were doing something relatively minor and, despite uniforms, did not confuse themselves with the nursing staff. In the old days, there had been trouble from time to time with a student nurse, but that sort of trouble had been easily settled. As a nurse one had some authority, an authority doctors recognized and respected. Nowadays? Well...

So Sally had gone into special nursing and then several years ago into the Willig Nursing Home. Once she would have thought of this as a big comedown, but the fact was she was paid more than she would be at the hospital, even for special nursing, and there was a similarity among her patients that made it undemanding work. Basically, although there was no need to be explicit about it, she was dealing with people who were waiting to die.

In the hospital, one worked for a cure and discharge and a return to normal life. There was no question of that at the Willig. These people weren't going anywhere, not ever again. Sad when you thought about it, so Sally didn't think about it much. She put in her time, thought of it as a kind of baby-sitting, drew her money, and left her patients' problems at the Willig when she went home.

Home was a one-bedroom apartment in the development on the east side of the Fox River. She had moved there after Arnold left, after she sold the house and set about beginning a new life. They would have been married ten years a month after the divorce. Sometimes Sally wished her marriage had not broken up before she and Arnold had reached a nice firm number like that. Better to be able to say she had been married ten years than nine years, ten months, and seventeen days. So that's what she did say, that it had been ten years. She also spoke of the divorce as if it had been an amicable agreement between adults. But she could still remember vividly the panic she had felt when Arnold told her. He had given her the news over the telephone, making it even more unreal. Just called up one day and said it was all over and he wasn't coming home again. There hadn't been a fight or anything, at least not recently. He said he had come to realize it just wouldn't work out.

"Where are you calling from?"

"What difference does it make?"

"I have a right to know."

"Sally, you don't have any rights over me at all, not anymore."

And he had hung up. A few days later a lawyer called. She got a lawyer too. She had never seen Arnold again, not to talk to. Just like that it was all over.

How alone she had felt. How rejected. How frightened. What would become of her? She had felt security in marriage. Arnold would take care of her. That's what husbands are for. Thank God, she had her nursing degree. The settlement made it sound as if Arnold would go on supporting her, and technically he was supposed to send her money every month, but that had stopped years ago, and she had no idea anymore of where he even lived.

She had her own realization, after that phone call. She had never respected Arnold. Oh, she had thought she loved him once, but hadn't it been more a sense of flattery, even of relief, that she would get married after all? She was twenty-six years old when they married, and it was a great comfort that someone actually wanted her.

She had dropped out of regular nursing. The great hope was that they would have a family. At least, that was Arnold's hope. She made certain it didn't happen. This was when she had gotten hooked on daytime television, during the first years of her marriage. And of course it was one of the great attractions of the Willig Home. Watching the soaps with the patients was part of the job. She particularly liked to watch with Mrs. Spaulding.

Mrs. Spaulding was in her nineties, beyond vanity. She did not like to have her teeth in her mouth and it was always a bit of a struggle getting the denture in place. She was such a sweet little woman, her white hair so fluffy and shiny. But when she got mad she swore like a trooper. This is not uncommon among the very old; Sally knew this. She knew what anesthetics brought out of the nicest people. But where on earth had Mrs. Spaulding learned such words? Most of the nurses at the Willig considered Mrs. Spaulding senile. So did her doctor, a very fat man named Skinner. Sally knew otherwise. She had assured Mrs. Spaulding's daughter that her mother had many lucid moments. Lucid hours. She loved the soaps and sometimes could keep track of their serpentine plots. If Sally had expected Mrs. Downs to be relieved by this information, she was disappointed. What a sourpuss the daughter was. This was Mrs. Spaulding's view too, and the things she called her daughter after she had been at the Willig to visit her mother! She had wondered where the hell her daughter was after the murder and Sally was happy to accept Dr. Skinner's decision that there was no need to tell the old lady her daughter had been butchered to death by her husband.

It was a little tricky making sure she didn't learn the dreadful truth from a television news program.

Early on in Mrs. Spaulding's stay at the Willig she had remarked on how much Sally reminded her of her daughter.

"In looks. You couldn't possibly have as bad a character."

Her lopsided little smile struck Sally as mean. Naturally she was eager to see what the daughter looked like. The comparison was flattering, thank God. Sally found it pleasant to believe she resembled the very patrician, very well-dressed Mrs. Downs, who swept through the nursing home as if she had just bought the place, lock, stock, and barrel, and was likely to fire anyone who did not look efficient. Of course she was equally struck by the differences. Mrs. Downs's nose was narrow and aquiline; Sally's was a little pink bulb. She also weighed more than Mrs. Downs but of course that was temporary. Sally always considered her weight to be wrong. It wasn't that she doubted the scale. Rather, she fully intended, sometime soon, to go on a diet and get back to her real weight. The fact she had not been the so-called "real weight" for a decade did not diminish her conviction that her current condition was a little lark she was on, nothing lasting. Nor was she as tall as Mrs. Downs. It occurred to her that Mrs. Spaulding had not meant her remark to be flattering. The old lady might very likely have said Sally looked like her daughter just to be malicious. Or had she said simply that Sally reminded her of Mrs. Downs? She had half a mind to ask. But she never did. After the murder of Mrs. Downs, it would have seemed bad luck to pursue the matter.

That was when she and the old lady had grown very chummy, when Sally was preventing Mrs. Spaulding from learning the awful news about her daughter. They played Scrabble at first, but Mrs. Spaulding was such a cheater, insisting nonsense combinations of letters were English words anyone must know.

"Are you an immigrant, my dear?"

"I was born in Fox River and I don't think 'quish' is an English word."

"Did I say it was English?"

Sally sighed and read the old woman the rules but it did no good. The soaps saved them. No need to play games when the baroque plots of those daytime dramas unwove perpetually before them on the screen of Mrs. Spaulding's magnificent color television.

Was Mrs. Spaulding so different from everyone else in the way she watched daytime television? When she confused people in the different dramas with one another, at least she seemed to think she was peering through a window at a single world. But she also interwove those televised stories and their characters with real happenings and real people. Her daughter and son-in-law, for example. Mr. Downs was a funny one, a tall drink of water who, after the death of his wife, before he was arrested, simply ignored all the No Smoking signs. Finally, when the way things were going was clear, Sally just left him alone. It was like granting the condemned his last wish. If he wanted to smoke, let him. Let him scatter ashes all over Mrs. Spaulding's room so that Sally had to clean up after he left and before Smitty got a look at it.

Felicia Schmidt managed the Willig the way Girl Scouts go after merit badges. She had been in the army and lived in the expectation that an inspection might be called at any moment and by God they were going to be ready for it. She was a pain, but Sally admired her. If you were going to run a place like the Willig, you ought to do it right. People were paying enough for it. The No Smoking rule was one you could argue about. It posed a problem for Sally, who had been trying to quit for years but still smoked her daily quota of filtered mentholated tasteless monstrosities. At the Willig she used Mrs. Spaulding's john for her smoke; any telltale odor of cigarette smoke could be referred to the lingering effect of Downs's visits.

Sally could have fallen over Thursday afternoon when he showed up. The paper had been full of the trial for days. This was the day the verdict would be given and everyone assumed he would be found guilty. And there he stood in the doorway of Mrs. Spaulding's room. Sally scrambled to her feet in confusion. Had he escaped? Had he come to murder her as well, because of her resemblance to his wife?

"How is she?"

Mrs. Spaulding, propped up on her pillows, had closed her eyes. They snapped open.

"Where on earth have you been, Howard? I kept telling this one here I wanted to see you but she wouldn't do as I said."

"I've been tied up." A wraith of a smile flickered over his thin face. He looked around for an ashtray and, seeing none, let the ash from his cigarette fall to the floor. Sally went to the bathroom and brought him back a glass. He thanked her.

"I want to be alone with Laura."

Laura was Mrs. Spaulding. "She can stay. We have no secrets from each other, Sally and I."

"Is that right?" Downs looked more closely at Sally and the fear that she had felt on first seeing him came back.

"We watch television together." It seemed such a feeble remark. She was glad to get out of the room.

It was a perfect excuse to telephone Casey, but when she did, there was no answer. She had never been able to reach him at the number he had given her. She rang the operator and asked about it. It was a genuine number.

Sally put down the phone as if she were hanging up on her hopes. She had always meant to ask Mr. Downs if he knew Casey came to see his mother-in-law. The second time Casey came to the Willig he and Sally had hit it off somehow. They talked and laughed and when he suggested dinner, she thought why not. They ate at the Casa Polenta and Sally pretended she liked the hot, heavy, spicy Italian food. For a month or so, once a week, sometimes more, he would come by the Willig. She went on about the place and he let her. You would have thought a big lug like that really cared about a nursing home for old people. He had met patients. Of course he already knew Mrs. Spaulding.

And then he stopped coming. No warning, no reason, he simply stopped coming. That had been about the time Mrs. Downs was killed. Sally wanted to ask him about it, since he had been associated with Mrs. Downs, but she never got the chance.

When she found out about the acquittal, she had the explanation of Mr. Downs's sudden appearance in the middle of the program Sally called "As The Stomach Turns" (to annoy Mrs. S.; she really loved it). It made her wonder if Casey, too, would show up again.

Now *there* was a pleasant thought.

But before it could happen Mr. Downs was arrested for the murder of his lawyer.

11

HE HAD sat with Michelle at the trial and the invitation by Farrell to come have dinner at the Casa Polenta was general enough so Gene Lane took it to include himself.

"We can go together," he said to Michelle. She wore a black suit with a flaming red scarf accenting it at the throat. Her jet black hair was pulled back and those lovely oriental eyes made it necessary for him never to look directly at her. His impulse when he did that was to tell her he loved her. So he did, debasing the coin, lowering it to the level of "Have a Good Day."

"Abjectly," he added.

"Are we invited?"

"Personally."

She looked at her watch. "I want to go home first."

"I'll take you."

"No. I have my car."

"When should I pick you up?"

"When does it begin?"

"I'll be at your door at six-thirty."

And that was that. God, he could have skipped down the corridor of the courthouse, past the priest who was talking with two men shorter than he, one with an unseasonal hat pulled low. He went down the stairs like Fred Astaire — is that where the name came from? If he had had a stick and a top hat, it would be perfect. He thought fleetingly of showing up at Michelle's in black tie. He looked good in formal clothes. And it would be at once a nice move and a bit of a gag. Gene Lane, the barrel of laughs. The *Pagliaccio* of the Downs Agency. His crack that Down's syndrome was a prerequisite for working there was tasteless, but he used it more often that he should.

Imagine old Downsie getting off with a not guilty verdict. The son of a bitch must have bought the jury. Farrell at least seemed capable of that, but he was good, very good. Watching the old phony at work in the courtroom, Lane resolved that the next time he himself was indicted for murder he would engage Farrell. The man could have gotten Judas Iscariot off. How had he managed to convince people, who must have been as sure as anyone else that Downs had killed his bride, that he should be pronounced not guilty? Downs had witnessed Farrell's performance and he still did not know. Such tricks he himself could use selling insurance, not that he was much of a slouch at it now.

Although he was single, Gene Lane lived in a three-bedroom house. It seemed a promise to himself that he would marry and have a family. He hated living in apartments. His house was on a two-acre lot on a bluff overlooking the Fox River and on a clear day he could see the Sears Tower in downtown Chicago. It did not occur to him that a prospective bride might feel like a bit of a prop being introduced to a house already furnished. How could she impose some touch of her own? Gene Lane assumed that a woman's hunger for security and being provided for would overcome any reluctance.

In early October the late afternoon sun filtered through the just changing leaves and there was an invigorating crispness in the air that made him regret he must return to town. He stood beside his car in his driveway and looked out over the expanse of his lawn. The first fallen leaves were scattered about. His mums were gloriously in bloom. He would have liked to get into his yard clothes and putter about. If Michelle were not going with him to that dinner he would forget about it. With an ambiguous sigh he went inside.

He made a bourbon and water and sipped it before hopping into the shower, where as always he sang "Over the Rainbow" off key. He had brought his drink into the shower stall with him. It seemed a definition of decadence, sipping an iced drink in a hot shower. Eat your heart out, Nero. The Roman might have had his choice of nubile mindless maidens, but Eugene Lane much preferred the prospect of winning the heart and hand of Michelle Moran with an honest proposal of marriage. He had her surrogate pop, Howard Downs, on his side anyway. Howard thought Eugene Lane was all right and not just in the insurance game. He gathered this from his manner. He treated him like a son. A quasi son-in-law. Alas, he could not ignore that parental approval is often the kiss of death. As for Michelle, she showed as much interest in Casey Janski as she did in him.

Casey. He was built like a linebacker. Or a hitman. Toweling his own pudgy body to a pinkish hue, Gene wondered if women were really attracted to men who look like gorillas? Not that Michelle had ever had a date with Casey. Nor were they excessively chummy at the metaphorical water cooler. The point was more dismal. She was as interested in Casey as she was in him, and she wasn't all that interested in Casey.

Lane's theory was that the whole business about Downs's refusing to get a lawyer was part of a scenario written by Farrell. And Farrell was a friend of Casey's. That had been clear enough beforehand, but if there had been any doubt of that it would have been removed by the celebration dinner at the Casa Polenta.

The restaurant was proof that when artistic taste is absent from an Italian it is totally absent. To call the Casa Polenta garish would be to suggest that it aimed at some standard and missed it. It had the charm of an ill-lit public restroom. The stucco was laid on so heavily, inside and out, that the place looked edible. These and other wry asides Lane poured into the ear of the divine Michelle when they arrived. She had changed into a black dress, a mysterious creation that seemed to involve overlapping panels. Jewelry? Pearls, period. Beautiful. On seeing her he suggested that they run away and live in sin together. She ignored such remarks but she took exception to his criticism of the restaurant.

"I like it."

"How can you like what you can't see? They should provide white canes at the door."

The table for the Farrell party was located under a spot embedded in the ceiling so one did have intermittent glimpses of one's fellow celebrants. Farrell, in a fever of triumph, seated people and nearly succeeded in separating Michelle from Lane. Clearly he wanted her next to him. Lane made sure he was on her other side.

It was a dinner that Lane, like everyone else, would describe *usque ad nauseam* to the police. Needless to say, he and Michelle were long since gone when the police arrived at the restaurant and discovered the body of Farrell out back. They were questioned at the office the following morning. Neither one of them had any idea either that Farrell was dead or that Downs had confessed to his murder. This was so much more baffling than Downs's acquittal that Gene Lane, for once in his life, was speechless. "This is ridiculous," Michelle said.

Lieutenant Horvath and Officer Lamb neither agreed nor disagreed. Gene Lane saw the two almost as old friends, given the interviews when the death of Mrs. Downs was under investigation. Witticisms, he had learned, were wasted on these two. Dull, straightforward answers were what they had wanted and that is what he had given them. No, he had no reason to think Mr. Downs would want his wife dead. He was told Howard was the beneficiary of her insurance. How much? One hundred thousand. Lane chuckled. As doctors don't take care of themselves and lawyers forget to make out their own wills, so insurance men seldom take their own advice about providing for the future you will not live to see. Horvath pointed out that it was different, a policy on a spouse. Lane decided not to say one hundred thousand was a laughably low amount. In any case, it would do little more than create tax problems for Downs. Public servants might not find that an amount to sneer at.

And now here they were, back again, with the preposterous statement that Farrell was dead and Downs had killed him.

"Why ridiculous?" Agnes Lamb wanted to know.

"He has confessed to it," Horvath said.

"Then he's protecting someone."

"Who?"

Michelle looked at Gene Lane, eyes smoldering theatrically, opening and closing her milk-white hands with their long lacquered nails. The Dragon Lady.

"Me?" Gene Lane asked. "You saw me slip away before dessert and do away with our host?"

The police already knew he and Michelle had been at the Casa Polenta the night before. And so it began, the endless questioning, repetition, the painstaking establishment of the fact that, crazy as it seemed, neither he nor Michelle had the least idea when the murder could have been done.

"Time of death is after midnight, before two."

"We left after midnight," Michelle said.

"And before two," Lane added.

Despite the long session, he kept remembering things later that he had not told them. How had they failed to see Farrell leave the table when Michelle was immediately next to him and Lane next to her? Because when the dancing started, after the meal, people took whatever seat they wanted when they returned to the table. Long before midnight the original seating had been discarded. Something Casey had said to him seemed significant now, Lane did not know how. They had been in the men's room. Casey said, "I'd like to have seen the look on Mrs. Spaulding's face when she heard that verdict."

"Who's she?"

"Spaulding," Casey repeated.

"I heard you the first time. I don't know the lady."

"She's Downs's mother-in-law."

"Ahh. I see what you mean. Well, a lot of people will resent the verdict."

"Resent it?" And Casey Janski had exploded in laughter.

12

"Look, why don't you record this session, then we won't have to keep going over and over the same thing. If you want to waste your time, that's okay. But it would leave me free to work. I have to earn a living."

"The last thing we want to do is waste time, Ms. Whitmore." Agnes Lamb's voice was a purr and Cy recognized her pleasure when she knew she was breaking through the cool of Phyllis Whitmore. "I suppose things are pretty scrambled around here with the boss back in jail."

"If he is in jail, it is his doing, not yours."

"I know. We can't confess to murder for him."

"He is no more guilty of this murder than he was of the last one."

"Why do you suppose he confessed to it?"

"You'll have to ask a psychiatrist that kind of question."

"You think Mr. Downs is mentally ill?"

"No. Except in the sense that everyone is, or so they say. What I meant is I am not going to get into that kind of analysis of the man I work for."

Cy said, "Good enough. Let's go back to the events in the Casa Polenta last Thursday evening."

"Oh my God."

Cy couldn't blame her. They had taken her through it half a dozen times, getting essentially the same account on each occasion, the variations about what you would expect. Phyllis Whitmore had parted from Downs in the courtroom with the understanding that she would attend the celebration dinner at the Casa Polenta. Her impression of Downs was that he was drained from the experience of the trial, relieved to have it over with, and still a bit stunned by the outcome.

"Where did you spend the interlude before dinner?"

"Right here." She looked around the office with a possessive expression. Queen of all she surveyed? That hypothesis had made sense when they were dealing with Mrs. Downs. The death of Farrell confused everything. It made no sense whatsoever. Unless Downs was crazy and wanted to throw his life away he would not have jeopardized his freedom so soon after regaining it or, having killed Farrell for whatever reason—and the reason he had given Keegan and Dowling was the one he had stuck with and Horvath could not believe it—he certainly would not have rushed back to jail.

"Where did Downs go?"

"I don't know. Not here."

They knew he had gone to visit his mother-in-law, even though Downs himself had not mentioned it. Agnes had turned it up when she checked out Downs's mother-in-law and was told by Sally Wise about the visit. Did it matter whether or not Phyllis Whitmore had known of that? Would it matter if she had known and denied it?

"Have you asked Mr. Janski?" Ms. Whitmore said.

"Why him?" Agnes wanted to know.

"No reason. He might know."

"Do you think something happened between the closing of the trial and the dinner at the Casa Polenta that explains why Downs killed Farrell?"

"I haven't any idea. But then, I don't think Mr. Downs killed Mr. Farrell."

■ 81 ■

"Did you always call him Mister?"

"I don't understand." But she straightened her shoulders and her eyes grew bright with wariness. Cy nodded. It was time they socked her with the affair she had been having with Downs.

"When you were with him socially. After work."

Agnes leaned toward the woman, poised, probably hoping the suggestion would be denied so they could lead her into a host of denials before confronting her with unassailable evidence that she had been the mistress of her boss.

"Howard and I were lovers for almost a year."

'So you should know more than Mr. Janski about how he might have spent his time before the dinner." Agnes had not skipped a beat. There was no sign in her manner that she had played a big card and not won the pot. "It is because your relation with Mr. Downs is more intimate that we find questioning you most useful."

Phyllis Whitmore's face had become a taut mask, the corners of her mouth dimpled in a cold smile, and she avoided the eyes of her questioners. "I had expected that to come out in the trial."

"There was no need for it. Downs's bloody fingerprints made the search for motives relatively unnecessary."

"It is even less necessary to bring that up now, is it not?"

"We're not accusing you of anything," Agnes said sweetly.

"Had you and Mr. Downs gone to the Casa Polenta on previous occasions?" Cy asked.

"Not often."

"But you did go there?"

"He liked Italian food."

"There are lots of Italian restaurants."

"Going there the other night was Mr. Farrell's idea."

"You heard him suggest it?"

"It was his party."

"Perhaps he asked Mr. Downs where he would like the celebration to be and he suggested his favorite Italian restaurant."

"If he did, I didn't hear him."

That was the little crumb that came out of the repetition of questions. They had been accepting Downs's suggestion that the choice of such a restaurant had been Farrell's. He had been condescending toward the whole idea of the Casa Polenta. To learn now that he had been there before, and that his girl friend did not reject the description of it as Downs's favorite Italian restaurant, made Horvath's afternoon. He left Phyllis Whitmore to the tender mercies of Agnes and headed for the Casa Polenta. Gino Figlio was barely civil when Horvath came into his office.

"Watching you on the screen, Horvath, I got bad news. You'd never make it as a cop on TV."

Figlio referred to the set in the corner, which now showed a shot of the empty hall down which Horvath had just come to Figlio's office.

"Was Farrell a regular here?"

Figlio nodded. "He ate here, sure."

"Once a month, once a week, what?"

"Maybe every two weeks."

"How about Downs?"

This time a shrug. "About the same."

"Was he always with the same woman?"

"The one who was here the other night?"

"Her name is Whitmore."

"I know that now. Yeah. Always the same woman."

"How about Janski?"

"Who's he?"

"He was at the celebration dinner too."

Figlio shrugged. "So?"

Cy settled back and Figlio frowned. Like Phyllis Whitmore, he was fed up with all the questions. They had the man who said he had done it, why the hell didn't they leave other citizens alone?

"We wouldn't want to convict an innocent man."

"Not even if he confesses?"

"But how did he do it, Gino? Nobody here saw a thing. Nobody in the kitchen saw two men go through. So how did Farrell's body get outside in an enclosed yard? There some other door to the back?"

"No."

"Let's go take a look."

Figlio shook his head. "You want to take a look, take a look."

The area behind the restaurant, enclosed by a high cinder-block wall, inevitably covered with stucco, was as wide as the building and half again as deep. Horvath stood on the step of the door that opened onto the back area from the kitchen and looked around. It was a totally enclosed space. There was no gate or door in the surrounding wall. There was only one way into that yard. He went back to Figlio.

When he came out of the kitchen, he was farther from the door of Figlio's office than when he entered this hallway through the beaded door from the dining room. It was while walking toward the mounted camera that the idea struck him. He did not take a chair when he re-entered the office.

"The people in your kitchen are lying when they say they saw no one go through the kitchen and out that door Thursday night."

"You want to think it, Horvath, you think it."

"I've decided to prove it."

"You found something?"

"We found Farrell's dead body out there."

Figlio looked disappointed or maybe relieved. "So you didn't find anything."

"Let's say I just remembered something." Horvath pointed at the television set where the empty corridor outside still appeared. "You say that thing records as well as films?"

"Anything it takes it records, sure. Automatic."

"On what?"

"On film."

"Where is the film for last Thursday night? Anyone who came from the dining room and went toward the kitchen would have been photographed by your camera, right?"

"By God, you're right!"

"So let's find out."

"It will have to be developed."

Figlio could have told him to go to hell. Or at least to go get a warrant and by the time he was back with it, the film could cease to exist.

13

MICHELLE ALWAYS imagined she could hear the ocean coming and going on white sand when she spoke to her mother in Florida. This was completely fanciful, since her mother lived half a mile from the shore on a man-made canal bordered by the closest thing to Midwestern grass Florida could provide. Her neighbors had boats, expensive toys, in which from time to time they would sail down the canal into real water, but Mrs. Moran's dock was only an ornament, like the lawn. All that, it seemed, was about to change.

"You're getting a boat!"

"Shelly, I've been *given* a boat. It's not as though I'm buying one."

Only her mother called her Shelly and she accepted it as she would a Lenten penance.

"Who on earth would give you a boat?"

"Believe me, you cannot be any more surprised than I am. There's money, too. Quite a lot of money. Shelly, I am one of Mrs. Downs's heirs!"

Mrs. Downs! What had been rushing through Michelle's mind was that Howard Downs had given her mother a boat in an attempt to transfer to her his own enthusiasm for sailing. Before a minute or two had passed she came to see that, in a sense, it *was* Howard who had given her mother the boat. Surely he would have been behind naming Yolande Moran a beneficiary of one of his wife's insurance policies. The money amounted to one hundred and twenty-five thousand dollars plus the boat, which, from her mother's description of it, must be worth at least as much again.

"That was very thoughtful of her," Michelle said carefully. "I had no idea you were so close."

After a long pause, her mother said, "Oh, I'm sure Howard is the explanation."

"Howard? But why?" She could not feign surprise. In high school she had briefly dreamed of becoming an actress, but try-outs for one play had been enough to convince her she could never imitate feelings she did not have.

"Because he is such a good good man."

Her mother spoke with the conviction of a witness at a canonization process. Michelle did not mean to mock this near-worship of Howard Downs. Far from it. The emotion she herself felt was not skepticism but envy. When she realized this she flushed with shame. How awful not to react to this wonderful news with the same simple hero worship her mother had for Howard. Over one hundred thousand dollars and a boat besides! He had been generous in the past, but this was amazing. Surely such generosity sprang from feelings more profound than benevolence. And now there was no Mrs. Downs as impediment.

Only Phyllis Whitmore.

The following day, all the while the police were talking with Phyllis Whitmore, Michelle wanted to cheer them on, but the snatches of conversation she heard whenever she passed the office suggested they weren't getting much from her. They had been at it for over an hour when the black policewoman, Officer Lamb, came out and asked if she could have a cup of coffee.

"Of course. I was going to come in and ask if you wanted some but I didn't want to interrupt."

"Interrupt what?" Lamb said, sighing. "That woman belongs on Mount Rushmore."

"He's protecting her," Michelle said, her voice scarcely a whisper.

"What did you say?"

"Mr. Downs. He said he did it because he thinks she did it. He's protecting her."

'Do you think she did it?"

"Yes!"

"She committed both murders?"

Officer Lamb meant Mrs. Downs and Vincent Arthur Farrell. Michelle nodded, but she felt like a fool because the policewoman was looking at her so skeptically.

"You were at the restaurant. How did she kill Farrell?"

"That's what you have to find out."

"You like Mr. Downs a lot yourself, don't you?"

"Mr. Downs is an old friend of my family," Michelle said, tipping her head back and looking straight at Officer Lamb.

"Is that why he hired you?"

"That was not the only reason. I could have found a job in many other places." But she was blushing and that made her angry. It was important the police know that Howard was innocent and that Phyllis Whitmore was far more likely to be responsible for those deaths. Michelle did not know how she had killed the people. The police were supposed to be able to discover things like that.

"How did Mr. Downs like the celebration party Farrell threw for him?"

"Mr. Downs is not a party sort of person. In many ways he is shy."

That had seemed the explanation for his failure to go beyond a platonic relationship with her mother. Howard had needed affection — he certainly didn't get any at home by the looks of things

—and it would have been far better if he had become, well, friends with Mrs. Moran rather than with Phyllis Whitmore. None of these terrible things would have happened if he had done that. If he had not done it, it was out of a sense of decency. Michelle was sure of that. Perhaps he hadn't thought Mrs. Moran would respond to that sort of proposal, from a married man, no matter what he might have been able to convey about the unhappiness of his marriage. In the same way, he had treated Michelle as if she were made of something other than flesh and blood. Which seemed too bad when she imagined Howard and herself. What a partnership they would have made. Officer Lamb wanted to know if Michelle had anything like evidence for what she was saying about Phyllis.

"Don't you believe in intuition?" Michelle asked.

"Not while I'm working. I'll take a cup of coffee in to Lieutenant Horvath."

"Keep after her."

"Sure. You're next."

Her remark must have had some effect on Officer Lamb despite that parting flippancy. An hour and fifteen minutes later Lieutenant Horvath and Officer Lamb were still interviewing Phyllis. Unable to control her curiosity, Michelle brought a cup of coffee in to Phyllis. The office manager and junior if not youngest associate was visibly relieved by the distraction.

"Work is piling up while we waste time," Phyllis said to Lieutenant Horvath. "Surely you must see now there isn't anything I can tell you."

"You're being very helpful and cooperative," the Lieutenant said, as if he had all the time in the world and meant to spend a significant portion of it right there in Phyllis Whitmore's office.

"Lieutenant, I do have rights."

"You do indeed. I reminded you of them at the outset. Do you want to have a lawyer sit in?"

"That isn't what I meant. You cannot question me endlessly."

"It is much nicer talking here than downtown," Officer Lamb said.

"I can have a warrant made out," Horvath offered.

Phyllis rattled her cup back into its saucer but her voice was calm in the way a taut string is motionless. "There is no need for a warrant and I do not require a lawyer. I repeat that I will do anything to help you disprove Howard Downs's ridiculous claim that he murdered Vincent Arthur Farrell."

"Good." Horvath looked at Michelle.

"Thank you for the coffee, Michelle," Phyllis said.

Back at her desk, Michelle told herself that the police had already suspected Phyllis. They had no need of her silly accusations. It could only be a matter of time until Phyllis said something that would tell them what they wanted to know.

"They still at it?" Mr. Janski stood in the doorway of his office, having just opened the door soundlessly. Michelle had forgotten he was there and she reacted to his question with a start. He nodded in the direction of Phyllis Whitmore's office.

"They're into their third hour with her."

"Then they're just fishing."

"What do you mean?"

"If they had anything, they would go right to the point."

"Have you been down to see Howard yet?"

After a pause during which he just stared at her he said, "What's the point?"

"Would they let me in to see him?"

"I don't know. You could try. Tell them you're from his office. Take some papers along for him to sign."

"Mr. Janski, why did he do it?"

"Kill Farrell?"

"No! Why does he *say* he did it?"

Mr. Janski stroked his face with a hand that seemed twice as large as any hand Michelle had ever seen. His eyes were a light, watered blue and looked as if he wore contacts but he didn't. When he looked at her he seemed to be an observer from a different world.

"Gallantry."

"Then you think she did it too?"

"Don't quote me."

Michelle got to her feet. The papers she would take were the office copies of Mrs. Downs's insurance policies. As she stuffed them into her briefcase, she began to wonder if Howard would agree to see her. He had vetoed her visits when he was on trial for his wife's murder, but that didn't mean he'd refuse to see her now. Now was completely different.

It was absurdly easy. A very nice policeman named Officer Pianone took her up to the top floor of the courthouse where the jail was.

"You a relative, Miss?"

"I work for him."

Pianone nodded. The flesh around his eyes seemed to be holding them shut. He reminded her of a trained animal counting with a toss of its head.

Michelle said, "Do you know Officer Lamb?"

Pianone's tiny eyes grew smaller. "Why?"

"She is at our office now with Lieutenant Horvath, interviewing."

"Horvath's okay."

Michelle had thought mentioning his colleague would please Pianone and his reaction surprised her.

"I don't know if they're making much progress."

The elevator had reached the top floor. The door slid back and Pianone started out, then stopped and indicated she should precede. Apparently he had changed his mind. He remained in the elevator. She turned just as the doors closed on him and his beady little eyes stared hostilely at her. It seemed Officer Lamb did not have an admirer in Pianone.

"Someone is with him now," the officer behind the desk told her. The lid of one of his eyes drooped in a way Michelle did not like.

"May I ask who it is?"

"Sure. I'll even tell you. A priest. Father Dowling."

Howard and the priest with him looked like twin cases of anorexia nervosa. The priest was Father Dowling and Howard seemed surprised she did not know him.

"I thought you were a member of his parish, Michelle." The twinkle in his eye might have been malicious, but it was hard to tell. Howard, in proletarian blue dungarees, looking for all the world like a workingman, was seemingly at ease despite his unintelligible claim to have murdered Vincent Arthur Farrell. Michelle found her boss even harder to read than usual, but that might have been due to the presence of the priest.

Michelle asked, "What is your parish, Father?"

"Saint Hilary's."

She was about to say that she went to Mass at Nativity but she did not. For one thing, that was so seldom true now, it would have been misleading; for another, it would have been to play Howard Downs's game, whatever it was.

"I spoke to my mother last night," she said.

His eyes widened slightly, then flickered toward the priest. Aha. But she refused to take the hint.

"She is overwhelmed by your generosity, needless to say."

Howard turned sideways on the chair as he crossed his legs. This had the effect of half turning his back to her. Spanking clean work shirt, a table containing nothing but an ashtray, above them a preternaturally white light. Howard said to the priest, "Mid-westerners should not move to Florida. Michelle's mother has not been the same since she did. But nothing I could say would persuade her to stay."

Michelle just looked at him. If it had not been for Howard, her mother wouldn't be in Florida at all.

She and the priest were seated side by side, facing Howard across the table, and when Father Dowling looked directly at her, Michelle had the feeling his eyes opened on depths wherein the meaning of life might be concealed. "Are you related to Howard?"

"I work for him." It seemed Judas-like to reduce her relation to that of simple employee. She added, "Howard and my mother are old friends."

"I knew Michelle's father," Howard said, and his tone made it clear he meant to terminate the topic. "What's in the briefcase, a file?"

"As a matter of fact, yes. But not the kind you mean." She got out the Manila folder and handed it across to him, causing the guard who had been lounging against the wall like a cigar-store Indian to stir. Satisfied that she was giving Howard only papers, he subsided into suspended animation. After the ease with which she had brought the briefcase in, it seemed a bit tardy to wonder about its contents now.

Howard ruffled through the papers without any apparent interest. His eyes lifted to the priest. "It is amazing how boring business affairs look from the vantage point of jail. To think that I have spent my life on nonsense like this." He let the papers drop to the table.

"Getting and spending," the priest murmured, and Howard nodded in apparent comprehension. Michelle thought it might be a scriptural allusion. "I imagine it's a good deal like being on retreat."

"Retreat?"

The priest explained to Howard what a retreat was. A day or two or three of withdrawal from the world, in a monastery or some religious house: silence, prayer, reading. Peace. A chance to let the crust of daily life dissolve and the real self emerge. That could be a disturbing experience, he added. Howard nodded as if he knew.

Michelle remembered a retreat she had made as a sophomore in college. There had been a vague thought of a religious vocation, but mainly she had wanted to take spiritual inventory. The experience had been at once pleasant and disturbing and she had never repeated it. Now Howard's interest in what Father Dowling was saying, his agreeing that, yes, being in jail was something like that for him, excited her. Perhaps the excitement was due to Howard's heretical dismissal of those papers as unimportant. Their lives and fortunes were built on such pieces of paper, on columns and columns of numbers and, ultimately, the bottom line. If Howard began to doubt the importance of all that, where would it lead? Michelle could not stop herself from putting that question to him.

He smiled at her, a more serene Howard than she was used to. "To sea, Michelle. Out to sea. I would like to sail away and spend weeks, months, just bumming around in my boat."

"You'd die of boredom," Michelle said, as if to exorcize the pull of Howard's dream.

He looked at her. "Maybe you're right."

But it was obvious he didn't for a minute believe it.

14

"WHAT DO you know of Michelle Moran, Phil?"

"Only what I read in my reports. Why?"

Keegan's cigar smoke mingled with the smoke from Father Dowling's pipe and the rectory study was filled with a blue-gray cloud that, at least to the pastor's senses, seemed pleasant. Marie Murkin had just appeared in the doorway, holding her nose and making exaggerated gestures with her free hand, waving away the smoke.

"Is anyone there?" she asked nasally.

Father Dowling ignored her. "I met her today at the jail when I was visiting Howard Downs."

"She works for him."

"There's cherry pie," Mrs. Murkin said. She was no longer holding her nose.

"Not while I'm drinking beer, Marie," Captain Keegan said. Father Dowling, too, declined.

"Oh, I knew you wouldn't have any," she said to the pastor. "But I was counting on Captain Keegan."

"Later, Marie," Phil said, as if making a concession. Cherry pie was his favorite, as Marie well knew.

It was a mark of Phil's status in the rectory that he could thus address so independent a housekeeper as Marie Murkin. Marie imagined she would prefer Father Dowling to be as

■ 95 ■

demanding as Phil, to have his appetite and appreciation for her cooking, but doubtless she would find him taxing after a time. Meanwhile she complained that cooking for Roger Dowling was like cooking for a Trappist. The pastor of St. Hilary's could not deny that he simply ate whatever she put before him. Doubtless his childhood upbringing explained that, at least in part. The Depression had not been a time to develop fancy tastes, let alone gourmet ones.

"Michelle Moran brought some business papers for Howard Downs to see."

Keegan nodded, frowning. He did not see much point in the remark, obviously. Dowling was not sure himself what the point was, but the somewhat coded interchange between Downs and Michelle Moran had nudged his curiosity. He pushed the cards across the table for Phil to cut.

"She has a mother living in Florida."

"Who does?"

"Michelle Moran. I wonder what connection there might be between Howard Downs and the Morans."

"I'll check on it," Phil said, watching like a hawk while the priest dealt. The two men had been playing cribbage together for years, Keegan knew his host was honest as the day is long, but he could not let anyone deal cards without keeping a sharp eye on him. Once in the service, in a game played on a blanket laid over the tiles of a barracks shower, Phil Keegan had lost a month's pay, and he was ever after convinced he had been cheated.

"Downs obviously knows the mother."

"I said I'd look into it."

"Maybe Agnes Lamb already has."

Keegan scowled. "Or Horvath. Either way, I'll get the report."

Roger Dowling did not blame Phil for wanting to put the Downs matter out of his mind, at least for an evening. Phil had been convinced Downs murdered his wife; now he was convinced the man had not murdered Vincent Arthur Farrell. He was not the kind of policeman who was content to get a man he considered guilty on any charge he could. If a man who murdered his wife was wrongly acquitted and then found guilty of killing a lawyer he had not killed, Keegan would not think that, however sinuously, justice had been done. The priest was not sure that justice is often done, but he knew Phil disliked such theoretical discussions and he did not mean to spoil the evening by introducing one. He was willing to wait to see what the police turned up on Howard Downs and the Morans.

In the meantime he pursued a little inquiry Phil could not. Michelle Moran's name was in the phone directory and the address put her within the boundaries of Nativity parish. André Conway, a silver-haired, silver-tongued man a few years older than Roger Dowling, was pastor of Nativity and more than happy to talk to his fellow priest.

"Why don't we have lunch, Roger?"

"I say Mass at noon."

"Afterwards, then. I'll come by and pick you up. Have you ever been to Le Bleu Canard?"

"Have you ever eaten at the Saint Hilary rectory, André?"

"Please. I want to take the opportunity to escape rectory food. Over a good lunch I will tell you all I know."

"I will buy your lunch, André."

"Of course you will. What was it you wanted to talk about?"

"A young lady named Michelle Moran."

"Yolande's daughter! Where on earth did you come across her?"

Conway's apparent ignorance of Michelle's current activities did not mean the lunch would be uninformative, but Roger Dowling was less hopeful than he would have liked to be. If nothing else, he could catch up on archdiocesan gossip. André

Conway was a bottomless well of information on the real or alleged doings of the cardinal.

When Roger Dowling emerged from the side door of the church at twelve thirty-five, a gleaming sedan was parked outside the house and beside it stood Marie Murkin, her hands hidden in the sleeves of her sweater, listening to Father Conway explain to her the advantages of his automobile. You would have thought he was trying to sell it to the housekeeper.

"I *could* make her a good deal on it at that, Roger. I only drive it to church on Sundays."

There was velvet on the collar of Conway's black cashmere coat, which he wore capelike over his shoulders. His hair was longer, more theatrical, than it had been when Roger had last seen him. Marie clearly did not know quite what to make of this priest who carried himself like a celebrity. Was it fair to André to imagine he was displaying his profile to imaginary cameramen?

Marie said, "I still don't see why you don't eat here."

"Father Dowling thought you needed a day off," Conway said, not realizing the remark would unsettle Marie. If she took a day off in a month it was a miracle, and any suggestion that the rectory could continue to operate in her absence brought on a mild depression. Now she looked suspiciously at Father Dowling.

"Father Conway wants to eat at Le Bleu Canard, Marie. His mother was French and he still has a great appetite for snails and frogs and tripe."

"Tripe?"

"The large intestine, Marie. Well cleaned, of course. It reminds me of white chocolate before it is cooked."

Marie's mouth fell open at the revelation of such debased appetites.

"I always wondered what tripe meant." She made a schoolgirl's face.

Le Bleu Canard had the look of a tea room to Father Dowling, with its diminutive square tables, ladder-back chairs, light pastel colors. The hostess, a very tall woman with a severe profile, displayed protruding teeth in recognition when they came in.

"Ah, Monsieur l'abbé, it is so good to see you again."

André took her hand and for a split second Roger thought he was going to kiss it. Perhaps he was put off by the several pounds of jewelry it bore.

"Antoinette, this is Father Dowling. His is a most demanding palate. I told him your chef is *cordon bleu* and he replied that he would be the judge of that. I say this in prudent warning."

"You will not be disappointed, Father," Antoinette assured him as she led them to a table in the corner.

It took some persuading to convince Conway that he did not want wine with his lunch.

"You *never* drink?"

Conway's tone was one of shock.

"You make it sound awful."

"It is awful. How can you digest your food without wine?"

"I'm a medical miracle."

"Roger, I'm serious. If you don't want to drink, don't. I never touch liquor myself. Dreadful stuff. But wine is the essence of civilization. It is an integral part of the meal. You must have at least one glass."

Roger managed to order Perrier water despite André's missionary efforts, but he feared he had spoiled his guest's lunch.

"You must remember that you are half French, André."

"I never forget it. French and Irish. What a recipe."

"Isn't Yolande a French name?"

It took a moment or two for André to take the hint. "Ah. Very well. You want to hear about Yolande Moran. I understand. I will earn my lunch."

Yolande Moran had already been a widow when Conway

was appointed pastor of Nativity and Michelle was just a girl.

"How long have you been at Nativity?"

"Ages." He had to think. "Fifteen years. Is that possible? We grow old, Roger." But there was a saving incredulity in his voice.

The Morans, mother and daughter, had been left well-fixed by the husband, apparently. Yolande had never worked and Michelle had gone to the best schools and done extraordinarily well.

"I wonder what has happened to her," Conway mused.

"Don't you know?"

He did not, and he was a bit ashamed to learn she still lived in his parish. The address was different and that softened the blow somewhat but, together with Roger's refusal to take wine, it left André puzzled and a little defensive.

"What do you know of Howard Downs, André?"

"The man in the paper?"

"Is that your only knowledge of him?"

Something flashed in André's eye but he quickly concealed it with a lidded look. "Don't tell me he's in my parish too."

Roger Dowling laughed. "He's not a Catholic. He is a friend of the Morans. I had hoped you would know him."

"Roger, this is just between us." Conway leaned toward Father Dowling. It was his habit to invoke confidentiality whenever he passed on some news. "Yolande was a very attractive woman. For all I know, she still is. She was not an unmerry widow, if you catch my meaning. There were suitors. Beaux, as they used to be called. I had expected another marriage, but it did not happen. Perhaps she suspected they were after her money."

"Was Howard Downs one of her unsuccessful pursuers?"

André's brows shot up and he smiled. Touché.

"Michelle Moran works for him."

"For Downs?"

But Conway let it go at that, and Roger Dowling began to fear that Conway would tell him nothing more despite this expensive lunch. The mineral water was good, and while he did not find the crêpes addictive, he enjoyed those too. But he had hoped to learn something useful for Phil Keegan.

In the end, it was the wine that did it. Conway had poured the last of the bottle and was savoring a mouthful when he lifted a finger and his eyes shone. He swallowed.

"Downs! Downs. Of course. Roger, there *is* more."

"I had hoped there was."

Conway, obviously ready to divulge information, was not eager to do so without drama. He sipped his wine again, eyes crinkled in a smile. He grew serious. "Roger, I must ask you to take what I have to say with the deepest sense of responsibility. It has the potential to hurt people grievously."

Roger assured his fellow priest that he would treat anything he was told as a sacred confidence.

Even at that, Conway hesitated, but it seemed obviously histrionic. "I must be certain that I did not first learn of this in the confessional."

Roger waited while Conway, head tossed back, eyes closed, reviewed his memories. At last his eyes snapped open. "No. I am morally certain I did not learn this under the seal." He sat forward. "Roger, you are correct in suspecting there is a special relation between Mr. Downs and the Morans. He was indeed a suitor. And more than a suitor."

"I see."

"Precisely. They might have married if there had not been the impediment of a Mrs. Downs already in place. But the affair did not end there. You realize I am speaking of matters that antedate my own acquaintance with the Morans."

"I understand."

"Of matters that antedate Michelle. Roger, she is the child

of the illicit union between Yolande Moran and Howard Downs."

Conway sat back in his chair, as if exhausted by this revelation. The dramatic terms he used contrasted with the earthier idiom other colleagues might have employed. This conferred a romantic flavor on the remark.

"Are you sure?"

Conway solemnly nodded his silver head. "I am sure."

It was easier to pay the bill after Conway had told him about Michelle. Had André remembered it all along, holding it back for dramatic effect? Roger could believe it. He had been told Conway once took half an hour to convey the news of the last papal election to a classmate, eking out the information so that his listener had the sense of being present in the Sistine Chapel during the voting. André was perfectly capable of dissembling throughout the meal in order to produce a bombshell at the end.

"Drop by my place, Roger. I'll get out the parish records on the Morans."

"Good enough. By the way, what does *bleu canard* mean?"

"You're pulling my leg."

Roger Dowling imitated a duck, to his own surprise. Being with André brought back memories of youth, the inanities of seminary life, horseplay and wordplay, and all the rest.

"You're quacking up, Roger."

"It comes from paying through the bill."

15

PHIL KEEGAN was reluctant to admit that it made a great difference that Michelle was Downs's daughter, but the priest was so obviously pleased to pass on the information he could not say, "So what?"

"Does she know?"

Roger Dowling could not say. Did even that make a difference, one way or the other? If it did, Phil Keegan did not find himself inclined to find out.

"I can't very well just ask her," Roger said. "And you mustn't either."

At the outset of the conversation Phil Keegan had given Roger the Scout salute when the priest asked him to treat as confidential what he was about to tell him. Roger should know better than to think a cop would not use whatever knowledge came his way if it helped him to do his duty.

"No need for that, Roger. We'll check her birth certificate."

"I've already done that. And Father Conway showed me the baptismal certificate as well. In both cases George Moran is given as the father."

"A dead man?"

"It was possible she had been conceived before he died."

"What did George die of?"

Roger Dowling beamed. "It would be easy for you to find that out, wouldn't it?"

Sure. It was always easy to get diverted from a job at hand and dig around in the past for facts of doubtful relevance. Intriguing as Michelle Moran's parentage might be, Keegan did not see how it would wipe the Mrs. Downs and Farrell murders off the slate. Nonetheless, he told Roger he would get blood samples and test out Conway's claim. Neither Downs nor Michelle need know.

Surprisingly, Roger vetoed that as unethical. He was opposed to testing people without their knowledge or consent. He seemed well informed on the subject. Apparently people have been enlisted in research projects that were systematically misdescribed to gain their assent. Deception. Keegan found the example disturbing. He himself had used deception more than once, and he was sure he would again.

While Roger Dowling had been canvassing the clergy for clues as to what might lie behind Howard Downs's preposterous claim that he had killed Farrell, the police had been pursuing the slogging routine that nine times out of ten produced the solution to crimes under investigation. Keegan had come to the St. Hilary rectory from poring over the reports Cy and Agnes Lamb had made of their interviews. Roger should know of these, lest he think the investigation was going nowhere. He began with the one they had conducted with Michelle Moran.

"Lamb sums it up by saying she has a crush on her boss and is convinced Phyllis Whitmore lies behind most of the evil in the universe."

"Are those Officer Lamb's words?"

"That is their drift." Phil cleared his throat and frowned. He regretted using the fancy phrase. But it was the remark about Michelle Moran's attitude toward her boss that bothered Dowling. Even if Roger's information was correct — and Keegan had doubts about anything whose source was the Reverend Father André Conway — Howard Downs would know, even if Michelle Moran did not, and could be expected to act, or not to act, accordingly. Keegan found it a pleasant thought that a daughter would unconsciously recognize and admire her father. Thoughts of his own daughters, scattered across the country, busy with their families, tugged at his heart. He loved to see them, but to visit them and be condemned to days of doing nothing other than being a guest was more than he could bear.

The upshot of the interview with Michelle was that she knew nothing of the murders and was too negative toward Phyllis Whitmore to be a reliable source of information.

"Whitmore is another matter. It is interesting to compare the interviews with her held when we were investigating the murder of Mrs. Downs and those Cy and Agnes conducted yesterday. Agnes Lamb proposes Whitmore as a suspect in both cases. As for Farrell, she had as much opportunity as anyone else at the restaurant. Discussions of her affair with Downs turned up the fact that she had a key to his house."

"What on earth for?"

"Roger, they were having an affair. She admits as much now. The question is, how long did she have the key?"

"What is her answer to that?"

"She doesn't know we know she has such a key. While she was being interviewed in her office at the Downs Agency, her apartment was given a thorough search. Don't look shocked. We obtained a warrant. Impressions were taken of keys she kept in a table beside her bed. One of them is a key to Downs's house."

"I suppose there are dozens of innocent explanations of that."

"Name half a dozen."

"Well, given her confidential role, he might have given her such a key routinely. More important, he could have given her the key after the murder of his wife. So she could look in on things while he was in jail."

"That's possible," Keegan said gruffly. It wasn't fair to lead Roger on, but frankly, he was a bit ticked by the way the priest presented the Michelle Moran stuff as the clue they had been unsuccessfully seeking.

"It doesn't make much sense to say she used such a key on the occasion of Mrs. Downs's murder and then kept it in a bedside table."

"It does if someone else knew she had it."

"Howard Downs?"

"Yes." Keegan filled his mouth with smoke and let it trickle from the corners of his mouth, his eyes on the priest. He wanted Roger to be in a receptive mood for Agnes Lamb's hypothesis. If he told Roger and was not taken seriously he would be out on a limb, and he preferred to avoid that. "Consider this, Roger. Downs goes to trial for the murder of his wife. He never admits doing it, but he really didn't do much to save himself either."

"That's true."

"And he was as surprised as the rest of us when Farrell got him off. Imagine what a relief that must have been to him. Yet within twenty-four hours he turns himself in as the murderer of Vincent Arthur Farrell. Why?"

"Because he hadn't killed either?"

"That's right. Now, why would anyone do a thing like that?"

"I think you'd rather tell me."

"To protect someone else."

"Ah."

"That ties them together, doesn't it? It makes some kind of sense out of Downs's behavior."

"Who is he protecting?"

"The woman with whom he was having an affair."

"Phyllis Whitmore?"

"I know, I know. Initially implausible. Why would anyone lay down his life for Phyllis Whitmore? Agnes Lamb has an answer. When it comes to their attitude toward women, the stupidity of men knows no bounds. You and I may think Phyllis Whitmore isn't worth it, but that is no test at all of what Howard Downs might do. We don't love her."

"Phil, I grant that's an ingenious theory and it does seem to cover everything. But it simply does not match my sense of Howard Downs. I wager I've spent more time with him than Agnes Lamb has."

"It *was* an ingenious theory, Roger."

"I don't understand."

"It is no longer just a theory. We found something else in Phyllis Whitmore's apartment. We found clothing with bloodstains that match Mrs. Downs's type. A blouse, a skirt, a pair of stockings. They had been washed, of course, but there are ways of bringing out latent stains..."

"Did you test all her clothing?"

"Not quite."

"What on earth led you to do that?"

"I've been telling you. Agnes Lamb was pretty damned persuasive. At least Cy thought so. You know what I think of theories. So I got that warrant and put a team of investigators to work. Now it is no longer a theory."

"Well."

"Is that all?"

"I congratulate you. And Agnes Lamb. But I still don't understand how her theory provides a motive for Phyllis Whitmore to kill Vincent Arthur Farrell."

"It doesn't." He might just as well be frank with Roger. "But if we are able to pin Mrs. Downs's murder on her, we ought to be able to put together the other pieces of the puzzle."

Even as he said it, Keegan did not like the speculative tone of his remarks. The best that could be said was what he had already said: Phyllis Whitmore had as much opportunity as anyone

■ 107 ■

else at the restaurant to kill Farrell. "Yes," Roger Dowling agreed. "But I should think she had far less motive. After all, he had just won an acquittal for a man she loves and a man, if you are right, who had been on trial for a murder she herself committed. It seems a curious way to show her gratitude or relief or whatever the appropriate emotion would have been. What it could scarcely have been is a desire for Farrell's death."

"It is extremely odd, Roger. And I will not appeal to the irrationality of women in love."

"As Agnes Lamb's theory depends on the irrationality of men in love?" But Roger smiled when he said it. "I suppose you mean to arrest Phyllis Whitmore."

"First thing in the morning."

16

THE BODY of Phyllis Whitmore was found in her office at the Downs Agency the following morning.

She was at her desk and had fallen forward onto it so that her hair drifted out across the scattered papers like a giant inkblot. The glass from which she had drunk lay on its side a few inches from her lifeless hand. Whether or not it had been self-administered, or unknowingly self-administered, she had died due to an overdose of sleeping tablets.

Horvath got there only minutes after the boys from the mobile lab and he kept out of the way while they did their stuff. It was not often that the scene of a murder was previously familiar to him, but he had spent hours talking with Phyllis Whitmore here and could not help wondering if there was a connection between those lengthy interviews and the lifeless body sprawled forward across the desk.

Lamb on the phone had been unable to conceal her disbelief. "Why do you say murder?"

"You know what she was like."

"The heat was on, Cy. People crumble. Has suicide been ruled out?"

Suicide had not been ruled out. Nothing had been ruled out. He did not begrudge the admission, particularly when it would enable Agnes to enjoy her day off. Well, maybe "enjoy" was not the right word. But from her point of view, it made a lot more sense that Phyllis Whitmore, convinced they were closing in on her guilt, decided to sip her way into oblivion.

Cy didn't believe it.

He had learned things since he and Agnes questioned Phyllis Whitmore that made matters increasingly complicated. First, there was Keegan's mention of the fact that Michelle Moran could be Downs's daughter.

"Could be?"

Keegan gave him the short form of his conversation with Roger Dowling. Horvath did not share the captain of detectives' purported indifference to this. Sure, he knew André Conway. Sure, the documentary evidence — birth and baptismal certificates — told against it, but as Keegan admitted, that only figured. A good deal of Keegan's attitude was due to reluctance to admit he had ever been substantially helped by Roger Dowling. Cy Horvath knew better. And this information was dynamite.

"What do you make of it, Cy?"

"I'll have to think. What about a blood test?"

"Go ahead."

"No need to let Downs know, is there?"

"Not as far as I'm concerned."

For Michelle, he checked her personnel folder at the insurance agency while he was waiting for the lab people to finish in Phyllis Whitmore's office. Type O. He also learned there was no file on Downs here. Why should there be? He was the big boss. He got the lab technician they called Brillo aside and asked him if he could get a blood sample from Downs without causing a fuss.

"Say no more." Brillo tried a Bela Lugosi look, but with his wild hair-do it didn't work.

The second bit of information had come from Figlio last night. When Cy got home, his wife told him a man had phoned and wanted his call returned no matter when Cy got in. It was Figlio.

"You got a projector, Horvath?"

"No."

"I'll bring one. There. I don't want you coming around here."

Figlio parked around the corner from the house and walked up the street, arousing every dog in the neighborhood as he did so. He looked shaken when Horvath opened the door.

Inside, he thrust the large carton he was carrying at Cy and looked toward the closed door. "This goddamn neighborhood is like a jungle. Those dogs."

"It would be worse without them."

Figlio thought about it. "Maybe." But there was deep doubt in his voice, as if he would prefer mugging to being attacked by dogs.

They set up the projector right away. Figlio said nothing and Horvath did not quiz him. The fact that the man had brought the developed film was sign enough there was something on it.

And there was. Horvath had expected the film to have the same clarity and resolution as the screen in Figlio's office, but it was a grainy, shadowy image that was not helped by the fact that they projected it right onto the wall of the living room.

There had been a lot of traffic in the hall that night and Figlio volunteered no comments, speaking only when Cy asked him to identify someone or to stop the film. There seemed no possible doubt. None of those who took part in Farrell's celebration had been filmed going into the kitchen.

"Because they didn't go into the kitchen," Figlio said.

"There is no way they could have gotten in there and avoided your camera?"

"Horvath, you've seen the set-up. There's no way. So I'm

clean and my place is clean. I'm cooperating but I don't need any publicity about that. Keep the film. It's a big nothing."

"A big nothing," Horvath agreed. "You want me to walk you back to your car?"

Figlio hesitated before saying no and Cy stood on his porch listening to Figlio being barked back to his car. He closed the door and put the reel of film in the refrigerator. Figlio was right. The murderer had not been filmed.

But far more significant was the fact that Vincent Arthur Farrell himself had not been filmed going into the kitchen.

Neither the murderer nor the murdered had gone down that hall under the watchful eye of Figlio's camera.

And that meant the back yard of the restaurant could not be as enclosed as it seemed.

Cy had known all this before getting the call about Phyllis Whitmore. That call deflected him from going to the Casa Polenta as he had intended. Now the information about Michelle Moran and Howard Downs made things more complicated still. In the circumstances, the death of Phyllis Whitmore seemed almost a diversion rather than a central event.

First, however, came routine, and Phil Keegan arrived to help with the third set of interviews with the associates and staff of the Downs Agency. The checkout book revealed no other late workers. Phyllis Whitmore had been alone in the agency from 5:15 the previous afternoon. The probable time of death was midnight. Before she had consumed the lethal dose of sleeping pills, she had drunk deeply from the gin in the bar in Downs's office.

Question: Where did the sleeping pills come from? It did not seem likely either that she kept a bottle of sleeping pills at work or carried them around in her purse.

Question: How long had she had a prescription for sleeping pills? The label on the bottle was from the Kunert Pharmacy and the doctor was Sopor. There seemed no alternative to sending Pianone.

"Where the hell is Lamb?"

"It's her day off."

"Her day off?" Keegan did not understand the notion of a day off. "Has she been told what happened?"

"I talked with her, yes."

"And she is still taking the day off?"

Agnes Lamb chose that perfect moment to appear in the doorway of Phyllis Whitmore's office.

"Has she been taken away?"

Agnes meant the body. Cy nodded. Agnes Lamb was not used to the sight of dead bodies. Cy did not think she would ever get used to it. Her obvious relief that the corpse was gone served to explain why she had not come even earlier. Keegan frowned and cleared his throat, the equivalent of a twenty-one-gun salute.

That was when Cy told them both about Figlio's film. He had to point out the significant fact.

"Then how the hell did Farrell's body get into that back yard?"

"I was going to take another look this morning. I'd like to go now."

"You think we can trust Figlio not to have doctored that film?"

"We can have it looked at. He gave me the reel."

Keegan told him to go take another look at the back yard of the Casa Polenta.

An hour and fifteen minutes spent outside the wall enclosing the back yard of the Casa Polenta, plus one phone call to the coroner, cleared up the mystery of how Farrell's body had gotten to where it was discovered without the murderer or his victim entering the yard by way of the kitchen.

Farrell's dead body had been dumped into the yard, over

the fence. There was a road back there that reminded Horvath of the way alleys had looked when he was a kid: wheel tracks with a wavering ribbon of weed separating them. It led into the area from the street behind the restaurant, parallel to that on which the Casa Polenta stood. The fact that the road was little used made it possible that a close examination of those dirt tracks would tell them something. Horvath got through to Brillo and asked the lab men to meet him there with their mobile unit.

"Downs is O, by the way."

"Good. What do you know about testing for paternity?"

"I'm innocent!"

"Do you need whole blood from both parties?"

"Yup. Who's the other?"

Cy thought about it. "Maybe I can get it myself."

"Do you have a license?"

"To be a prick?"

"Ho ho. You going to wait for us there?"

"I'll be here."

17

TUTTLE HAD been unable to get anything like a confirmation of the commission Peanuts had relayed to him that morning in his office when his day began with the unnerving sound of Luigi Pianone's voice in his ear. He could go directly to the alderman's office and ask, of course. He could also scale the outer wall of the courthouse if he had suction cup shoes and a more obvious death wish. What boiled Tuttle was that Peanuts himself seemed to be avoiding him. Was this any way for a client to treat his lawyer?

Don't get me wrong, Tuttle would assure himself as he avoided his own eye while shaving. I would settle for the clear statement that my services have not been engaged and I am perfectly free to accept other and conflicting assignments. (The fiction that severe demands were made on his time was one of the reasons he could not look himself in the eye.)

On the other hand, drinking beer from the can and tilted back in the office chair his father had bought him before Tuttle was even out of law school, he told himself he would be willing to donate his time to discovering, prosecuting, and personally hanging the son of a bitch who had killed Vincent Arthur Farrell. Lawyers ought to stick together the way cops did.

It was the thought of the rigid, frigid, laid-out body of his late colleague that brought the sweat to Tuttle's brow. It was a violent time. It was a violent world. Officers of the court, counselors of the law, were as vulnerable as anyone else. More.

At the memorial service, held in the rotunda of the courthouse, Tuttle had sobbed audibly at the thought that Farrell had been cut down at the very moment of his greatest triumph.

"Lucky him," Mervel said. They had repaired to the reporter's quarters after the service in order to toast Farrell and themselves in fair-to-middling bourbon. "Better now than when he was in a slump. That is, better now than any other time in his career. Remember that, Tuttle. You get lucky, it may be a sign you're about to go."

"Who killed him, Mervel?"

"Downs confessed."

"He didn't do it."

"Why not?"

"Think about it," Tuttle advised. "You going to kill some guy who saves your life? It makes no sense."

"Unless you didn't want to be saved. And don't forget that Downs could have afforded the best lawyer in town. He ended up with Farrell because he didn't give a damn. Farrell was his ticket into a life sentence and Farrell blew it by actually gaining an acquittal. So Downs killed him."

"So why can't you keep a straight face when you say it?"

"Whoever killed Mrs. Downs killed Farrell."

"But Downs was guilty as sin. Remember the way he was found with his wife's body."

"Exactly," Mervel said. "Would a guilty man have sat there holding her dead body?"

"Maybe it was suicide."

"Like Phyllis Whitmore? How about her for your murderer?"

"Don't think I didn't think of her," Tuttle said, and it was true. They might not have made anything of Downs and Whitmore at the trial, but Tuttle had homed in on it within hours after receiving his ambiguous commission from Peanuts's father. For

■ 116 ■

two days he and Peanuts had tailed her. The third day, Tuttle had been working alone. The day she died.

Phyllis Whitmore was the kind of woman Tuttle did not like and vice versa in spades. It wasn't just that she was a career woman — what the hell, Tuttle's mother had worked; she had been in charge of the food line at Whitney Junior High at the time of her retirement — there was something else. Contempt. Snobbishness. Tuttle had felt drenched in ice-cold water after he had decided on the direct approach and called to make an appointment.

Michelle Moran answered when he phoned, and when he said he was interested in an annuity and she offered to help him with it, he wavered, to hell with duty. But it would have been a waste, Michelle Moran was not going to take a second look at Tuttle apart from his supposed desire to purchase an annuity. So he said he had been recommended to Phyllis Whitmore and he was put through to her. He had to practically beg her for an appointment, at which presumably he was going to give her his money. But he had insisted. He had been given the cold shoulder by experts and knew how to handle it. So she had fitted him in at the end of her afternoon appointments on the day, as it turned out, that she would die. It said something of what she thought of the appointment that she had not written it down. Posthumous information. If his name had been in her appointment book, if the police knew he was the last one to see her on the last afternoon of her life, well, he would have been passing the hours with someone other than Mervel.

"D'you ever smoke, Tuttle?"

"I never really had the habit."

Mervel nodded. He was a chain smoker. Howard Downs was a chain smoker too.

"I know," Mervel said. "Non-filters. Man after my own heart. And he has a lot to live for."

The remark brought on a bout of philosophizing, fueled by the bourbon, and, in Mervel's case, stoked by the unfiltered cigarettes he smoked one after another. Did money bring happiness? Was it really love that made the world go round? What does it all mean? Is death the end?

If Tuttle had sobbed in the rotunda, he was crying openly now and being drunk had nothing to do with it. He told Mervel there was nothing like the law to give you a sense of the fragility of life. Mervel countered with the claim that covering the sordid news of the city made one grateful for mortality. That is when Tuttle mentioned having been with Phyllis Whitmore only hours before she died.

"At the Downs Agency?"

"I made an appointment. I said I was interested in an annuity. True enough. I just can't afford one. So she said come, and I came and we talked."

"What was she like?"

"She was a bitch."

"I don't mean in general. I mean then. Just hours before she died. Was there any indication..."

Tuttle's regret at having mentioned this was eased by alcohol and the fact that Mervel was according him a deferential attention that had been absent from the earlier part of their session. In response to Mervel's question, Tuttle flipped back the Irish woolen hat he wore winter and summer and consulted the water-stained ceiling above. The reporter's quarters had a modesty Tuttle found comfortable. Next to his own office, he liked drinking here. In neither place was there need to think of going elsewhere when the definitive drunkenness came. One could sleep as and where one was.

He decided it would be fanciful to say that Phyllis Whitmore had exhibited any sign that she was in the final hours of her stay on planet earth. So he said it.

"Yes. I sensed it at the time without knowing what it was I sensed. Maybe her own intimation of immortality was similarly equivocal."

Mervel was taken aback. Tuttle was not. When drunk, his diction became eloquent. As inhibitions dropped away, the British actors in the B movies of his youth rose to the surface and used him as if he were a ventriloquist's dummy.

"How long were you there?"

"For perhaps twenty minutes I kept up the subterfuge. Then I revealed who I was. She did not at first catch the significance of my admission. I told her I had been hired by Alderman Luigi Pianone to find the murderer of Vincent Arthur Farrell."

"Don't let Pianone find out you're using his name in vain."

"It's true." But he let it go. He was not that drunk.

"What did she say?"

"She threatened to call the police. I suggested she must have had her fill of talking with them by now. That struck a chord. She had started to rise, but she fell back again into her chair. I told her I was well acquainted with Keegan and Horvath and their objectionable methods. She asked if I knew Agnes Lamb. Lamb was the one who got to her."

"Her bête noire?"

"Now, now."

"So you cursed the cops together. When did you leave?"

Tuttle's mouth opened and closed. He reached up and tipped his hat over his eyes. "Shortly thereafter," he said, closing the subject. He had just remembered something. He had not been alone in the agency office with Phyllis Whitmore. Another person had been there. A man.

A very large and powerful man.

18

WHEN HOWARD Downs sent word that he was withdrawing his confession to the murder of Vincent Arthur Farrell, Captain Keegan had the insurance agent brought to his office.

Downs was wearing his own clothes, a dress shirt open at the neck, a tweed jacket, loafers. Keegan wondered if he had ever before noticed the expensive jewelry Downs wore. The watch, the rings, and, bringing a frown of disapproval to the captain of detectives' brow, a gold chain necklace. There was a crease visible in Downs's designer jeans when he crossed his legs.

"What makes you think you're innocent?" Keegan asked, striving for a light note he was far from feeling. It gave him a pain in the you-know-what to have Downs or anyone else make a mockery of the system in which Philip Keegan was working out his salvation.

His frown deepened at the thought. Would Downs even understand his view of life? Keegan lived in a vale of tears, heaven was his destination, what he did in this life would determine his eternal status. Being a cop had to fit into that picture or he could not have remained one. Oh, there were days when things became so murky he wondered if there was any difference left between right and wrong, but probably everybody's life had moments like that. For the most part, Keegan liked the clean concepts that governed his life: innocence and guilt, crime and punishment, the duties imposed on one as a member of society.

It was hard to hang on to such clarity when he looked across his desk into the untroubled countenance of Howard Downs. Here was a man who, if he had not killed his wife, Keegan was a monkey's uncle, and Farrell of all people got him off. So Farrell saved his life and was killed and Downs said he did it. Now he had changed his mind. Why?

"Phyllis's death alters everything."

"In what way?"

"Oh, come on, now, Captain. You must have seen why I was willing to take the blame for Farrell."

"Explain it to me."

Downs took time to light a cigarette. Watching the man smoke reminded Keegan of how good cigarettes used to taste. It reminded him of when everyone smoked cigarettes. Now cigarette smokers knew what it had always been like for cigar smokers, people turning their heads, glaring at the offender, holding their noses. Keegan unwrapped a cigar and put it in his mouth. Downs got up and held his lighter to it and Keegan puffed mightily, filling the office with smoke.

"I was protecting Phyllis. It was much the same in the case of my wife's death. Phyllis did it, Captain. I came home to that grisly scene and was found in the circumstances you know. That the woman I loved had killed my wife drained me of all will to live. I could not have accepted any alternatives open to me. Have Phyllis prosecuted, jailed? That would deprive me of both wife and beloved."

"It would have been the same difference if you had been sent to Joliet."

"The same but different. I think you understand."

Gallantry? That was the motive Roger Dowling had rejected, perhaps too swiftly.

"By the same token, I could not seek acquittal. For Phyllis and me to profit from what she had done, to attempt to build our happiness on such a deed, was repugnant to me. I preferred a lifetime in prison to that prospect, much as I loved Phyllis. Farrell upset my plan of self-sacrifice. I could have killed him."

"But you didn't?"

Downs smiled a wispy smile, then dragged deeply on his cigarette. It crossed Keegan's mind that he would buy a package of cigarettes on his way home and see what they tasted like after all these years away from them. Cigars were different. For one thing, he did not inhale them. No more than Roger Dowling inhaled pipe smoke. Marie Murkin considered this denial laughable. "Inhale? Look at this room." And she would invite the two smokers to notice the density of the air in the St. Hilary rectory study. "We're all inhaling it all the time." Keegan now wanted to taste again inhaled cigarette smoke. The tobacco industry ought to pay Howard Downs a commission.

"No, I did not kill Vincent Arthur Farrell." Downs pronounced the triple name with mild sarcasm. "I despised the kind of man he was, it gave me pain to have such a lawyer, and his crowing after that incredible verdict was all but unbearable, but I did not kill him. Kill him." He repeated the phrase wonderingly. "Dear God, who ever thought I would associate myself with taking another's life."

"Why did she kill him?"

"Because he learned she had killed my wife. He actually had his minions ransack her apartment. They found there evidence that she had killed Gloria."

"What kind of evidence?"

"Clothing. Bloodstained clothing. The stains were from my wife's blood. He actually went about building up a prosecutor's case against her. Her itinerary on the day of the murder. All of it. Farrell was working on several such alternatives as part of my defense. The bastard was far more competent than I dreamed.

Of course, he was practiced in defending guilty people and his technique was to throw sand in the eyes of justice. Is that the point of the blindfold? But in the case of Phyllis he had not simply a plausible alternative to my doing it, he had the guilty party."

"He told you this?"

"No! He knew I would veto use of it."

"But he didn't use it."

"He felt he didn't have to. He was willing to take the risk. After all, there was the appeal. Farrell was quite willing to dedicate the remainder of his professional life to my wife's murder. If I was found guilty, and he expected that, no matter what he said later he would have his knowledge of Phyllis's guilt to fall back on with the higher court. He still had leverage after the acquittal. With me. If Phyllis had killed my wife and I was unwilling to defend myself, he concluded that I knew Phyllis had done it and was protecting her. Acquitted or not, that left me open to blackmail. That was his leverage with Phyllis as well."

"So he told her?"

"He told us both at the same time. Offhand. In his office just after everyone scattered in preparation for his triumphal dinner at the Casa Polenta. He took two minutes to tell us both what he knew of Phyllis."

"What was her reaction?"

"She seemed to think the fact I had been tried for the murder made it impossible it could be she. Farrell quickly disabused her of that idea. And that was it, really. He laid his cards out and then we dispersed. There was no big scene about it. We might have been three conspirators exchanging information. The threat of blackmail was implicit, not overt, but it was there. Maybe we were all still affected by the euphoria of the acquittal, I don't know. He told us and then we dispersed, each going in a different direction, and then we met again at the restaurant."

"How did she kill him?"

"I truly don't know. I only know she did."

"When did Farrell leave?"

"It was after I did." Downs sighed. "These are events we have gone over and over, Captain. You know enough to know I did not kill Farrell. That suffices for the moment."

Keegan did not tell Downs they already knew of the clothing in Phyllis Whitmore's apartment and that on that basis they had been about to arrest her on the morning she was found dead. Somehow that would have sounded more like an admission of fault than anything else. Nor did he tell Downs of what Horvath had found in the area that skirted the wall enclosing the yard of the Casa Polenta.

"Tire tracks, Captain. Hers. No doubt of it. Her car drove in and parked on the other side of the wall just opposite to where Farrell's body was found. A ladder was placed against the outer wall."

"The body was just dumped over the wall? That's quite a drop."

"It was lowered. There was roll of canvas in the trunk of her car. It looks as if she rolled him up in it and then let him down like a pulley. Then she pulled up the canvas, stowed it in her trunk, and drove away."

"But how did she get him into her car?"

Horvath looked away. "You know Brillo, the lab man? He sees no problem. Farrell was full of vino, he was a man, Phyllis Whitmore was a woman." Horvath's shrug seemed an imitation of Brillo's.

Keegan could imagine it. Particularly now, when he had talked with Downs. Phyllis Whitmore was dealing with a man who knew things that threatened her freedom. She would have been desperate. Killing Farrell had been risky and desperate, but then, so had killing Mrs. Downs.

"What do we know of Phyllis Whitmore, Cy?"

"She was a lot of woman. Big. Strong. She had to be."

"You think she did it?"

Horvath looked impassively at Keegan. "I would hate to have to explain away all that evidence."

Keegan had let him go. He knew how Cy felt. But he had detected in Cy a misgiving he himself had had. That bloodstained clothing in Phyllis Whitmore's apartment, plus the key to Downs's house, were stupidly convenient. And now the tire tracks and the roll of canvas in the trunk of her car. You had to think Phyllis Whitmore was trying to get caught.

"I apologize for the nuisance I've been, Captain," Downs said, putting out his latest cigarette. "And now I shall stop being one."

"A matter of curiosity, Mr. Downs," Keegan said, and Downs did not get up from his chair. "I'm told that Yolande Moran is the beneficiary of your wife's insurance policy."

"One of them, yes. Did Michelle tell you that?" It was difficult to tell if Downs had been surprised by the statement. He certainly answered without hesitation.

"Were Mrs. Moran and your wife close?"

"Not in recent years. We were once extremely close. Yolande and George were our best friends. He and I founded the agency together, you know. The policy goes back to those days. I suppose it's odd that we never changed the beneficiary." Downs smiled. "Insurance agents are a bit like medical men. They look after everyone but themselves."

"You and Yolande were very close?"

"That's right."

Downs waited, but Keegan could not go on. Goddamn it, this was stuff he had gotten from Roger Dowling and if the priest wanted to waste time with gossip he was welcome to it. So far as the Fox River Police Department was concerned, Howard Downs was a free man and could go out and sell all the insurance he wanted to.

19

HOWARD DOWNS was happy to accept Roger Dowling's invitation to dinner at the St. Hilary rectory, and Marie Murkin overcame any latent feelings she might have had about Downs's guilt in the matter of his wife's killing and promised she would prepare a feast.

"Don't go overboard, Marie. He's only an insurance man."

Marie dealt with callers at the rectory door and over the years she had developed an effective technique for sending unwanted salesmen and vendors on their way. But in recent years she had met her match in the telephone solicitor. It was not that the housekeeper was loath to be rude. Rudeness seemed to have no effect on these relentless disembodied voices, and slamming down the phone did not promise the same satisfaction as shutting the rectory door on importuners. Father Dowling suspected it was Marie's desire to get the last word that undid her with such solicitors. Nor did he underestimate Marie's share of ordinary human gullibility. Thus it was that recently she had found herself engaged in prolonged telephone negotiations with a representative of an insurance company. Marie did not need insurance. She did not want insurance. It mystified her that she could not convey these simple truths to her tormentor. To identify Howard Downs as an insurance agent should have been the kiss of death.

"And Miss Moran," Marie said sweetly. "I do look forward to seeing her. Is Captain Keegan invited?"

"No."

"Just the three of you, then?"

"Unless you'd care to join us."

She just looked at him. She might sit at table when Phil Keegan was here, that was different. It was one of the myths Marie lived by that she was just a simple rectory housekeeper who cooked and cleaned and knew nothing at all of parish business.

Roger Dowling had thought of inviting Phil, but his old friend had not been receptive to the news about Michelle's relation to Howard Downs and perhaps he was right in this. Not that Roger Dowling for a minute doubted the truth of what André Conway had told him. Perhaps Phil didn't either, not really, but Conway was such a flamboyant figure it was easy to discount what he said. The real question was: did Conway's revelation have any bearing on the deaths of Mrs. Downs and Phyllis Whitmore? For days Roger Dowling had been oppressed by the thought that Michelle's being the daughter of Howard Downs provided just such a nexus.

Puffing on his pipe, seated at his desk, an open book lying ignored on his lap, he had imagined dreadful things. Mrs. Downs and Phyllis Whitmore both represented impediments to the coming together of Michelle's true parents. He had imagined the young woman, desperate to bring her parents together, removing those impediments. It made sense that Howard Downs would sacrifice himself for his daughter, no matter how implausible Father Dowling had found the suggestion that he would do so for Phyllis Whitmore. When the body of Downs's mistress was found dead at her desk in the Downs Agency, Roger Dowling had decided he must talk with Michelle. He called and, on the basis of their having met at the jail, invited her to lunch.

"Do you know Le Bleu Canard? It is very nice. We could meet there."

The stern woman with protruding teeth remembered him, and Roger Dowling saw that this impressed Michelle.

"You mustn't think I am an habitué. I've only been here once before. With another priest. He knows your family."

"I only have a mother."

How tempting it was to simply deny that, but Roger Dowling could not presume Michelle knew Downs was her father. That was what he intended to find out.

"He knew only your mother and you. Father André Conway."

"Nativity."

"So you know him?"

"I know who he is."

"That's right. You're in that parish."

She put down her glass of water. "Father Dowling, you should know that I am not a very good Catholic. I don't go to Mass very often."

"You should, you know. And not because you're good. Because you're not. The churches would be empty if only the good came."

Michelle was visibly relieved when the waitress came and diverted them from further discussion of her religious practices. Roger Dowling didn't blame her. Perhaps she found it uncomfortable to talk with a priest about anything, let alone her soul.

"When you visited Howard Downs at the jail, you mentioned that he had been generous to your mother."

"He has taken care of both of us over the years. After my father's death, he managed things for my mother. My father had been in insurance too, not very successfully, I gather, and Howard had taken him into his agency. That was shortly before he died. All the while I was growing up he expected me to join the agency. I didn't know that. But that is what I did."

"You don't regret it?"

"Oh, no."

"These have been hard days for the Downs Insurance Agency."

She seemed about to deny it. Perhaps she thought his remark referred to financial matters. When she caught his meaning, she nodded.

"And now Phyllis. I can't believe it."

"Did she ever talk of suicide?"

"I just don't believe she killed herself, Father. Why should she? Everything looked golden for her."

"Because Mrs. Downs was gone and he had been acquitted?"

She nodded reluctantly.

"Did Howard Downs love Phyllis Whitmore?"

It cost her to say so, but she replied, "I don't understand it, but he must have."

"You didn't seem to take seriously his remark that he would like to get on a boat and sail away from everything."

"He could if he wanted to. I mean, he is well off. He and my mother could go sailing together. Mrs. Downs left her a boat too."

"Mrs. Downs?"

That was when he learned that Yolande Moran was a beneficiary of Mrs. Downs's insurance.

"Isn't that odd?"

"Not really. I'm sure it was Howard's doing. He took care of my mother like that. Financially."

"Financially."

Michelle Moran's eyes drifted away and soon she was really distracted by the clientele of Le Bleu Canard. She had ordered a glass of wine and a quiche and now held the stem of her glass with both hands.

"This place is lovely. I wonder what it's like at night?"

"I've only been here for lunch."

As the result of that lunch, Roger Dowling decided two things. First, Michelle was unaware of the fact that Howard Downs was her father. Second, if nonetheless she had killed Mrs. Downs and Phyllis, she was a young woman of diabolical cunning. Not finding the consequent plausible, he discounted the antecedent and enjoyed his lunch.

"Is your mother the beneficiary of other policies at the agency?"

She laughed. "The Mrs. Downs one was a fluke. I am sure it goes way back to prehistoric times."

Prehistoric meant before she was born. Perhaps it always means something like that.

Phil Keegan's news about the tire marks next to the outer wall of the Casa Polenta and the canvas found in the trunk of Phyllis Whitmore's car added to Roger Dowling's sense of relief. That relief lay behind the dinner at the rectory. They would celebrate Howard Downs's recapturing of freedom and, though only the priest would know it, Michelle Moran's removal from suspicion.

"But who killed Phyllis?" Michelle asked when, sated with Marie Murkin's roast beef, candied yams, mashed potatoes, and asparagus casserole, they had begun the pleasant task of reviewing the events of the past weeks. Howard Downs had just summed up what Phyllis had done and he was surprised by Michelle's question.

"Who killed her? She killed herself, Michelle."

"I know they say that. I just don't believe it. She was too relentless a person to take her own life. Besides, why should she now?"

The question embarrassed Downs and the priest thought it

was because of his presence. Did Howard imagine he had not heard of his affair with Phyllis or, having heard of it, that he found it the crime of the half century?

"Relentless? Maybe. But if I wanted an example of a relentless woman, I would choose that black police officer."

"Agnes Lamb," Michelle said, nodding agreement. "Isn't she something? I could half believe she drove Phyllis to take that overdose."

"She may have the same effect on me."

"Has she been talking with you?" Father Dowling asked.

Michelle answered. "Father Dowling, she's on your wave length. Do you know she actually expected me to let her rummage through our files so she could check out beneficiaries on our policies?"

"I suppose that would take forever."

"Not anymore. Gene Lane has put all that sort of data on the computer. It's not the difficulty. I think we have been more than cooperative with the police, no matter what Agnes Lamb implies."

"Amen," said Howard Downs.

Michelle said, "Are there any surprises in there, Howard?"

"Let's hope they're only pleasant ones."

Marie Murkin entered then with apple strudel fresh from the oven and after the mandatory oohs and aahs they subsided into a silence relieved only by the sounds of contented mastication.

20

IT WOULD have been an emotional roller coaster for a woman half her age, but Mrs. Spaulding took the ups and downs of her son-in-law's life with a laugh. Sally Wise figured that this was only partly due to senility. Old people's real feelings came to the surface easily and it was pretty clear that Mrs. Spaulding had a grudging admiration for her son-in-law and that it went back a long way.

"Anyone who can put up with Gloria is either a saint or an idiot. Well, he's neither, and that makes him a mystery, which is just fine with me."

He was pretty good to her, far better than many sons are to their mothers at that time of life. There were a lot of old people who did not have the comfort and care of the Willig Nursing Home, something Sally Wise did not let Laura Spaulding forget.

"You just want to sneak a smoke in my bathroom, that's why you hang around me."

"Now Laura, that's not true and you know it. I like being here with you."

"Don't they let you watch serials on the set in the lounge?"

Meanness was another thing that came out of old people, but Sally knew how to deal with that. She turned off the TV and plunked Mrs. Spaulding back in bed and gave her a powerful sleeping tablet. That would teach her to talk back.

But her heart melted when she thought of the old lady left

all alone, however comfortably. Howard Downs was back in jail almost before he got out.

It was because of Laura that she was as interested in the Downs case as she was. Honestly, she read every word that appeared in the paper about it. Just when it seemed to be subsiding, there was another death. Phyllis Whitmore. And before you could say Jack Robinson, there was Howard Downs himself, looking like a million bucks and asking how his mother-in-law was.

Sally assured him Mrs. Spaulding was doing just fine.

"I suppose you've been keeping up on my troubles?"

Sally nodded. "And now they're over."

He crossed his fingers.

"Mr. Downs, there's a question I want to ask you."

He had started toward Mrs. Spaulding's room but he stopped and turned to her, a little wary. No doubt he expected her to ask some stupid question about the trial or about being in jail.

"Once a man named Casey came here with you."

"Yes."

"Well, I just wondered how he is."

"I'll tell him you asked."

"Thank you."

And off he went. It was one of those conversations where so much more seems to have been said than was said. Sally was certain Mr. Downs understood her interest and that he would get the message to Casey. She hoped he saw that she was not the kind of woman who makes trouble for a man, clingy, that kind of thing. She just wanted to see Casey in an adult way, that was all. She was a big girl and would make no demands.

A big girl. Honestly, the way she had gained weight lately. She seemed to do nothing but eat. You'd think she'd burn off the calories, running around the Willig Nursing Home the way she did, but no. It had gotten so she no longer wanted to get on the scale in the morning.

Well, she would go on a diet. She would! And she meant a crash diet, starvation city, she was going to get rid of all this blubber and get back to the weight she should be. The prospect of hearing from Casey provided motivation. He was a very big man and no doubt wanted a woman he could see, but enough is enough. She could lose fifteen pounds and still be a very sizable person.

She imagined Casey asking her to lose twenty-five pounds and thought how easy it would be to do. For him. It was even more pleasant to imagine him saying he liked her the way she was. What the hell, he wanted a woman he could feel when he hugged her.

One thing was for sure. If he came back she was going to treat him so nice he wouldn't just go away again.

He telephoned her at home and you would have thought it had been only a few days.

"Long time no see," she said, and bit her tongue. It sounded like criticism and she didn't want it to.

"It has been a while. I don't suppose you're free tonight."

"I'm never free," she said sassily and held her breath. It was a relief to hear his chuckle. Men liked a forward woman.

"I thought we might get together tonight."

At her place. Sally was disappointed. She had hoped for dinner and a movie first, building up the mood, but she let it go. When you thought about it, the fact that he wanted to come to her place direct was pretty flattering.

When it rains it pours. That day at work a very nice man with a sandy mustache and very nice brown eyes asked to talk to her. Gene Lane. He said he was a journalist from out of town doing a piece on Illinois nursing homes and he would appreciate it if she could give him a few minutes of her time. He had already cleared it with Felicia Schmidt, the director, so Sally said sure, of course.

They talked in one of the smaller visiting salons so Sally could light up. Gene Lane smoked too and that helped. He got out a notebook and asked her how she had come to work at the Willig.

He was easy to talk to, and how long had it been since she had had someone so interested in her? He was fascinated by Laura Spaulding.

"I won't use her name, of course, but it would help if we just concentrated on one of your patients, Sally. So tell me, does Laura have lots of visitors?"

"She has one. When he's out of jail, that is."

He laughed and she said no kidding, and he wanted to know what she meant, and off they went on the Howard Downs business, about which she was by now an expert, and it didn't matter, she was on duty, Felicia Schmidt had okayed the whole thing, so she just took her time. They got along so well she was actually disappointed that he didn't get more personal. He was younger than she was by a few years, but what the hell, he was in a strange town. It took a lot of convincing before he would believe Howard Downs was the only one who came to see Laura. He had got it into his head that she must have all kinds of relatives.

"Some of us really are all alone in the world, Gene, hard as you find that to believe."

He didn't take her up on that, but after he was gone and she thought about it, having a smoke in Laura's john after having given her a sedative to shut her up, Sally imagined that Gene Lane had really come on strong and she had had to turn him down because she already had a date tonight. There had to be some way she could convey to Casey she had other guys interested in her too.

■ 136 ■

"A man named Lane interviewed me today for a piece he is doing on nursing homes. I had a little trouble keeping him on the subject."

She drawled the remark half aloud, studying her expression in the mirror. That, or something like that, is what she would say to Casey when he came by tonight.

21

GENE LANE's grandfather had a mystifying way of breaking up his contemporaries by saying from time to time "They laughed when I sat down to play the piano," and even after Gene had had it explained to him he didn't see what was so funny.

Nonetheless he used a variation of it. "They laughed when I set out to computerize the files."

There was software available for insurance agencies but Gene Lane developed his own program for the Downs Agency and it was a marvel even if he did have to say so himself. The fact was that Howard Downs even on his best day did not understand the full significance of the computer revolution. There was a generation-gap explanation, of course. Downs thought of the computer as a sophisticated adding machine or typewriter or anything but what could streamline the office work and make two-thirds of the staff superfluous. Gene Lane was damned lucky to get an okay for a desk-top computer, but it turned out to be sufficient for his purposes because it had a hard disk and a fantastic memory.

He had expected Michelle to back him up, but forget it. If she had any fault it was that she took her prevailing winds from Howard Downs and she sensed his indifference to computers long before Gene Lane did and trimmed her sails accordingly.

"Gene, we have a perfectly reliable and efficient system now. Who's complaining?"

"Who *complained* about the horse and buggy? That's not the point."

So he had decided, if I have to do it alone, I'll do it alone, and that had meant spending a lot of time doing work a secretary could have done if she had had some computer training. Maybe some of the girls could have done it, but the project had become so decisively his that Gene Lane determined to go ahead and get it done and then demonstrate to his astounded associates how business was done in the waning decades of the twentieth century.

Only that sort of painstaking working through the files could have turned up what eventually did. A project that had begun in secrecy became one that had to proceed without anyone knowing what he was doing. It began to show up when he had twenty percent of the data entered on the computer and he tested it periodically as he went on. Far from being a freak of the original sample, it was a pattern that permeated the files.

When he had eighty percent of the data entered, he tapped out one of the crucial names, instructed the machine to search, and watched the policy numbers form a column twenty-nine lines long on the computer screen.

With everything else that had been happening in recent weeks, it was no mystery no one paid attention to what he was doing. Janski had looked in several times before leaving at night and asked him what game he was playing. It was Casey's joke that Gene Lane spent half his day playing computer games in his office.

"They laughed when I set out to computerize the files."

When what he had found was inescapable, he thought of talking to Casey about it, but he ruled that out when he put a few questions to the computer. Whatever else he was, Janski was not a mere spectator of what had been going on in the Downs Agency.

Michelle? Dear God, the thought of giving her even a hint of what he had discovered filled him with pain. He knew what her reaction would be. It would be crazy to expect her to applaud him. Nice going, Gene. You've discredited the agency real good. That ought to be worth a bonus.

So he decided he would gather more information. He didn't know what the hell he wanted the information for anymore, but he would go on. So he called up the Willig and told Ms. Felicia Schmidt a cock-and-bull story and went out there and talked with the nurse who looked after Laura Spaulding in the hope that she would inadvertently reveal something. And he drew a blank.

Before it was over he wondered if it was safe being in a private room alone with Sally Wise. Talk about sending a message! Even if she had weighed a lot less, she would not have been a concupiscible object, but there was something obscene about an overweight woman that age all but asking a guy to come up and see her sometime.

After the shock of Phyllis's death he wondered if she had found out what he had, if that had been the basis of her special relation with Howard Downs. The computer made it easy, but anyone who had been at the Downs Agency as long as Phyllis and who gave two-hundred percent to the job the way she did must have gotten some inkling of what was going on. Had she used it as a wedge into Howard's affections?

Ho ho. Sure, funny as a rubber crutch until you began to think Howard could have resented something like that. Imagine he had reacted the way Gene Lane did when eventually he went to the Willig and had to put up with Sally Wise for an afternoon. Imagine a predatory female like that who had the goods on you besides.

Honest to God, if Howard Downs had not been in jail on the night Phyllis Whitmore died...

Michelle's excuse for not going out with him tonight was at least novel. "The old having-dinner-with-a-priest ploy? Last time it was lunch."

"But it's the same priest. Father Dowling."

"Do you need a chaperon?"

"Howard will be there too. Obviously you have not met Father Dowling or you wouldn't make a snide remark like that."

"Pardon my anticlericalism. I studied with the Jesuits."

"Loyola?"

"No, Payola." It pained him that she did not remember — not that he was surprised. "Well, give him my love. I shall spend the evening with my home computer."

He had indeed succumbed and bought one of his own. It was easy to while away the lonely evening hours, though he would get up from staring at the green screen with bloodshot eyes. He was still seated at his computer when the phone rang.

"Gene Lane?"

"Speaking."

"Sally Wise."

Good God! He had lied to her and her boss and said that he was from out of town and now she had tracked him down. The woman was worse than he had thought. He searched desperately for another lie but then she spoke again and he forgot it.

"I finally connected you with the Casa Polenta thing. I mean, you were mentioned in the paper and I read all about that case, as I told you, because of Laura Spaulding's son-in-law. For whom you work." It sounded like an accusation.

"That's right."

"So why the fun and games?"

"I *am* writing an article." He snorted, an effort at insouciance, but he was unable to convince even himself that it was a plausible lie.

"Are you alone, Gene?"

"Are you kidding?"

"Don't tell me you're married. I know better. I know all about you, Gene Lane. It turns out that we have mutual friends."

"Who?"

"You'll find out. We're coming there to see you."

And the phone went dead.

22

WITHOUT TELLING Phil Keegan, Chief Robertson made an informal announcement to the press that he was going to call the meeting, and Cy Horvath did not need to ask what his boss thought of Robertson's statement that he would kick a few rear ends and get some action on the epidemic of murders that had struck Fox River. Phil Keegan looked as if he had in mind a victim who could extend the list at least one more digit.

Mervel slunk into Horvath's office with the news, though he probably did not fully realize that the detective division had not yet been informed of the chief's plan.

"Pianone must have forgotten to cancel his request," the reporter said.

"What do you mean?"

"Luigi. He was madder than hell because Farrell's body was found at the Casa Polenta. He's some kind of silent partner or maybe Figlio is just one of the family. So to speak. Anyway, he had Tuttle looking into it for him."

Mervel seemed to be serious. If true, this would call into question the belief that Peanuts was the only dumb bunny among the Pianones. Tuttle!

The unsuccessful little lawyer was a constant presence around police headquarters and the courthouse, ever on the lookout for business and there was no law against that, but Tuttle ranked somewhere below the late Vincent Arthur Farrell in terms of ethics and competence. Even if Pianone could overlook Tuttle's methods, he should have known he was not likely to get results from a lawyer.

Peanuts and Tuttle were thick as thieves, of course, but this was not exactly a coalition of talent.

Mervel said, "Now that the Farrell mystery is cleared up by the Whitmore suicide, Luigi and Figlio can relax."

Horvath said nothing. Reporters are not in the business of giving information and he assumed Mervel was trying for some exchange. The reporter wanted to know if the police accepted that interpretation of the death of Phyllis Whitmore.

"The official ruling was death by an overdose of sleeping pills."

"Self-induced?"

"There was no evidence of foul play."

"And Howard Downs says she killed the other two. You think she was strong enough to boost Farrell's body over that wall?"

"The way it was done, you could have done it, Mervel."

"Maybe. But why would I do it like that?"

To make it look as if it happened in the restaurant? Maybe in the hope that someone in the kitchen would be less than convincing in saying they didn't see Farrell pass through? Maybe... It was the damned uncertainty that made the meeting with Robertson particularly unwelcome.

Horvath shooed Mervel from his offiice and joined Keegan on the way to Robertson. Keegan's face was set in a scowl.

"We answer his questions, Cy. That's all. We got three bodies and as far as the detective division is concerned they are all accounted for."

Cy nodded. Keegan was as unhappy as he was with the idea that Phyllis Whitmore had killed two men and then herself.

The prosecutor's office had sent a new low-level assistant, a young woman named Tracy, freckles, rusty hair, translucent blue eyes. She was talking with Agnes Lamb when Cy and Keegan arrived and the four of them gathered in the chief's outer office like a wagon train at sundown.

"Tracy what?" Keegan asked.

"Sioban Tracy."

"Is that Hebrew?" Agnes asked. She seemed serious and Keegan stared open-mouthed at her.

"Gaelic. I am supposed to register the prosecutor's surprise that I am here. We have no cases pending in the matter under discussion."

"Did the prosecutor receive an agenda?"

Tracy smiled. "No. He heard it from the reporters."

"Speaking of which..."

Mervel and his fellows, Ninian, the stringer from the *Tribune*, and Gert Fingeret from the *Fox River Shopper*, sidled into the office.

Keegan said, "What the hell are you people doing here?"

"The public's right to know," Ninian smirked. Gert clacked her needles and looked at Keegan over the rims of her glasses. At which moment Robertson's door opened and out came Wayne Hanson, the press secretary. He beamed at the reporters and then turned as Robertson appeared in his doorway.

The chief acknowledged the press, faced the other group, and spoke while fixing his eyes on a point somewhat above Keegan's head.

He didn't want what he said to be construed as public criticism of the fine efforts of the Fox River Police Department, especially its detective division, but he was sick and tired to find a new mysterious death on the front page every time he picked up a copy of... He hesitated, then settled for the generic "newspaper." He was not alone in thinking that the public had a right to a full and fast explanation of what on earth was going on when the wife of a prominent businessman, a local lawyer, and now an associate of that same businessman, died by other than natural means. While he had every confidence that the police were pursuing these inquiries with vigor, he wanted the public reassured that he personally was riding herd on the police and would insure there was no flagging of effort for any reason whatsoever.

"What sorts of reason did you have in mind, Chief?" Mervel asked in his characteristically insolent manner. "Political?"

Robertson affected a laugh. "I don't see what politics have to do with it."

"It's being said that Alderman Luigi Pianone lit a fire under you."

Keegan was beaming. He despised the press, but from time to time it afforded him something other than acute pain and this was clearly one of those times. Ninian wanted to know if Robertson was criticizing the prosecutor's office as well.

It went on from there and within ten minutes, Hanson called it off and got the chief out of harm's way. Keegan was buoyant on the way back to his office, striding down the center of the corridor flanked by Lamb and Tracy. He had invited them to lunch. Horvath had declined. Robertson's little session might have turned into a fiasco for the chief but that did not relieve Horvath's sense that they were far from having anything like a satisfactory explanation of the three deaths.

He sat behind his desk, spun in his chair, and looked out at Fox River through the slats of a Venetian blind. First, Mrs. Downs. Stabbed repeatedly, she had bled to death in her husband's arms. She had been a harridan and Downs's initial account of what had happened was so implausible that he was charged with his wife's murder. It had seemed an open-and-shut case. Horvath still thought they had tried the right person and got the wrong verdict. How did he know? He didn't. Nor was he appealing to hunch or instinct or the kind of theory Keegan rightly scoffed at. When you find a man holding the dead body of his wife and that man is covered with her blood and that woman was a bitch, it is a safe bet the man killed the woman. The burden of proof was on the doubter.

But Downs had been acquitted and then tried to take the blame for another death he could not have been responsible for. Nor could he have been responsible for the death of Phyllis Whitmore. So if the three deaths were connected and Downs could not possibly have been the cause of two of them, chances are he was innocent of the third as well.

So much for logic. The argument that led to suspecting Downs of his wife's death was neither stronger nor weaker than the argument that seemed to exonerate him.

But Downs remained at center stage because now he claimed Phyllis Whitmore had murdered his wife and that he had gallantly taken the heat. Plausible? The question no longer seemed important when they had the evidence of those tire tracks and the canvas in her trunk to link Phyllis Whitmore with the death of Vincent Arthur Farrell. Call her death suicide and you have the basis for Keegan's public front that there was nothing further to explain.

Brillo's confirmation that Michelle Moran was indeed, on the basis of tests admissible in court, the daughter of Howard Downs? An interesting fact, but what relevance did it have?

The fact that Yolande Moran was a beneficiary of an insurance policy taken on the life of Gloria Downs? But it turned out that the Morans and Downses had been friendly years ago and Downs had acted as financial manager for Yolande Moran since the death of her husband. Michelle would have been conceived during the first confused months of Yolande Moran's widowhood and Downs's concern for mother and daughter became more rather than less explicable.

Michelle Moran. Horvath had tried her out for the role of villainess, the not quite acknowledged daughter sweeping away the obstacles to the union of her mother and father. The difficulty was that Michelle Moran apparently did not know of her relation to Howard Downs.

Cy was almost sorry he had not accepted Keegan's invitation to join him and the women for lunch. Maybe if he acted as if they had something to celebrate he would come to believe it, but he didn't really think so.

The following morning, his wife heard it on the scanner and when he came back from jogging she told Cy of two new deaths.

"This one sounds like a lovers' quarrel, Cy."

"What was the man's name?"

"I wrote it down. Lane. Gene Lane."

23

MICHELLE TELEPHONED her mother, wanting her head to be filled with distracting semitropical chatter and the faint suggestion that life was meant to be lived under the untroubled sun in Florida.

Mainly, she simply did not want to think anymore about what was happening in Fox River. Of course she did not tell her mother about Gene Lane and that woman. Her mother had not known Gene and no one seemed to know the woman who had been found with him in his house.

The day had started so *normal*, more normal than in weeks, with Howard in his office and Casey Janski in his. And Howard had wanted to see her first thing. After referring in a vague way to recent events, he had looked at her kindly. "I want you to step into Phyllis's shoes, Michelle. You're ready."

Well, she was, and she didn't pretend otherwise. Not that she wasn't immensely flattered and pleased, but she assured Howard she would justify his trust in her. Did this mean she would be an associate of the agency?

"That is exactly what it means."

Which would make her the youngest associate. When she went to inform Gene Lane of this, she found he wasn't in yet, so she let herself into Phyllis's office, closing the door behind her. It seemed a bit ghoulish to look around the room like this, but it was going to be her office now and she wanted to think what changes she would make.

It didn't look much the way it had when Phyllis worked here. Many of the things that had made the room hers were gone, packed up and sent off to her brother in Oregon, who had not even taken the trouble to come for the funeral. It turned out he was Phyllis's heir.

"Well, one of them," Howard said. "It's embarrassing, but she put me down as beneficiary on a very large policy."

Michelle was not surprised, but she didn't know what to say that wouldn't be offensive. That was when she first realized Phyllis was honestly and truly out of Howard's life. The atmosphere of the Downs Agency would be very different now that the rest of them could stop pretending they did not know Howard and Phyllis were having an affair.

Was it possible Phyllis had killed herself because she saw that the dreadful things she had done, rather than bringing her closer to Howard, had alienated him forever? The poor woman.

Michelle asked Father Dowling to say a Mass for Phyllis, going to the St. Hilary rectory for the purpose. Mrs. Murkin, before she recognized Michelle, wore a frown that disguised her natural pleasantness.

"Of course," she cried, when recognition came. "Do come in." She turned and called down the hall, "Father Dowling, Michelle is here. Michelle Moran."

That was a bit embarrassing. Was life in the rectory so dull her visit was an event? Father Dowling appeared in his study door. If the housekeeper vexed him, he gave no sign of it.

"Just go right into the study," Mrs. Murkin urged, and the priest stood aside so she could.

When she was seated she looked around the room whose walls were bookshelves. A desk, several chairs and lamps, it was a very comfortable room, and Michelle found the lingering smell of pipe smoke pleasant. Father Dowling sat behind his desk. Thin, sharp featured, he should have seemed severe, but he did not. He waited for her to speak, but she was certain that if her being at ease required it he would have been chattering like her mother. Well, not like her mother.

When Michelle told him she wanted a Mass said for Phyllis, Father Dowling smiled. "I hope Father Conway doesn't think I am luring his parishioners away from him."

"I would like to come to the Mass you say for Phyllis." It seemed a way to make up for her unkind thoughts about Phyllis.

"How about tomorrow noon?"

"Fine."

That had been yesterday. Now she had been chosen to succeed Phyllis. That seemed even more reason to have the Mass said for her.

There was a tap on the door and when it opened Howard was standing there. Michelle was embarrassed to be found looking over her new office so soon. Howard's solemn expression increased her unease.

"Stay seated, Michelle. There's been some dreadful news." He himself took a chair and looked around, almost bewildered. "More dreadful news."

"What is it?"

His eyes settled on her. "How well did you know Gene Lane?"

"How well *did* I know him?"

"He's dead, Michelle. He was found dead at his house with some woman. She too is dead. My God."

"Who is the woman?"

"They have not identified her yet, apparently. Lieutenant Horvath called. He is on his way over here."

"What for?" Hadn't they had enough? The thought of Horvath and Lamb spending more time questioning everybody was more than she could bear. Anger enabled her to put off for a time the realization that Gene Lane was dead.

"They will think we know something that can help them understand why he would do such a thing."

"What did he do?"

A suicide pact? Michelle began to shake her head even as Howard told her what he had heard from the police. It had been hard to believe that Phyllis Whitmore would kill herself, but it was impossible to think Gene Lane would. And with a woman? Michelle was sure she would have known of any woman in Gene Lane's life.

"Why would you know?"

"We went out a few times."

"But it wasn't serious, was it?"

"Nooo." She hadn't thought so, but Gene Lane certainly had. Could a man pursue her as he had while all the time carrying on with another woman? Michelle tried out the obvious and cynical answer to that question, but she didn't believe it.

When she went to St. Hilary's for the noon Mass, she had more than Phyllis to pray for. Gene Lane's death was even sadder than Phyllis's.

She knelt halfway up the nave, on the right, and precisely at noon Father Dowling appeared and the small congregation rose to its feet. The priest blessed himself with great dignity and concentration and Michelle felt herself being drawn quickly and naturally into the ritual. In fact, she was soon so much back into things, that distracting thoughts claimed her.

She had escaped from the office before the police had finished with Howard. Dear God, how repetitious it all seemed. Officer Lamb and that big likable hunk of a Horvath patiently asked question after question as if there had to be a clear explanation of everything. Michelle had taken refuge in Gene's office. Having been in Phyllis's office when the news of Gene came, she wanted to think of this new development while sitting at his desk. Morbid? A little, perhaps, but after all, she was half Irish.

So she sat at Gene's desk, touching nothing, looking at the neatly arranged papers, everything in its place. She had turned slowly, to face the small computer. Its dead screen stared at her blankly.

At Mass, in St. Hilary's, it was Gene's computer she thought of. She felt bad for not having backed him up when he argued the importance for the agency of computerizing their operations. Michelle agreed with him. She had made the suggestion herself, shortly before joining the agency, but Howard's reaction told her it would be useless. As far as Howard was concerned, there were enough machines in the office as it was.

When she went up to communion, she realized Captain Keegan was also at Mass. For a fleeting moment she had the thought that he had followed her to Mass, but he obviously had no idea she was there.

Back in her pew, making her thanksgiving, praying for the repose of the souls of Gloria Downs and Farrell the lawyer and Phyllis and Gene, Michelle made a little resolution. Before she went home tonight, she would go again into Gene's office. She would turn on the computer and check out the work he had done in recent months. If would be a kind of tribute, like playing Taps.

It would be interesting to see the results of all his labors.

Meanwhile she called Florida and talked to her mother and wished she was lying on a beach with the surf slowly rolling in and slowly rolling out.

24

ROGER DOWLING heard of the two most recent deaths from Phil Keegan when his old friend joined him for lunch after the noon Mass. Phil was quite visibly dumfounded by the latest development.

"Roger, it seems crazy to link this last thing with the Downs business, but it turns out the fellow worked for Downs."

"You say it was a suicide pact?"

"Note and everything."

"No mention of the Downs Agency?"

Phil shook his head. "It's one hell of a big coincidence. If I worked there, I would be nervous as a cat. But all they complain about is the fact that we want to ask them a few questions."

"Michelle Moran was at Mass just now."

"Is that right?"

"The Mass was said for her intention. The repose of the soul of Phyllis Whitmore."

"Was Whitmore a Catholic?"

"I don't know."

Phil stared at him as if he thought Masses for non-Catholics were a waste.

"Who was the woman?"

"She worked at a nursing home. She was ten years older than Lane. Her name was Wise. Sally Wise. She was fat and he was lean."

Nursery rhymes. Phil seemed nostalgic for a time when life and its puzzles could be overcome in doggerel.

"What nursing home?"

"The Willig. That place by the river."

"I know it."

Two former parishioners of Father Dowling's now lived at the Willig. The anteroom of eternity, as he had fancifully thought of it when he first went there, but the same thought came when he visited hospitals. He paid more attention to nursing homes. It was a somber thought that he himself might one day end in just such a cheerful, tidy, unreal place. But Felicia Schmidt was a good soul. Though Methodist, as Phil might say.

"Did I tell you about that idiotic announcement Robertson made the other day?"

"You did."

"Can you imagine what he will say now?"

"Nothing, I hope. He cannot seriously think the existence of the police force is a guarantee that such things will not happen."

"And that we will clear them up and get convictions."

"Now, who would you prosecute for a suicide pact?"

Soothing as he might be with Phil Keegan, Roger Dowling was himself more than struck by the connections between the deaths of the past weeks. And by the unsatisfactory nature of the received explanations of them. After Phil had gone, the priest went into his study where he opened the *Summa Theologiae*. After lunch he would read his breviary or St. Thomas or Dante and today was the turn of Aquinas. He was reading the Treatise on Justice, in part to make up to Phil for seeming to mock the detective's trust that laws and courts and cops assured that justice would be done. Perhaps it was, at least in part. In any case, Father Dowling had resolved to be instructed by St. Thomas Aquinas on the matter.

It was while he was reading of judgment and whether it is licit to judge another that, quite irrelevantly, he decided to pay a visit to the Willig Nursing Home. As soon as he completed his self-assigned reading. But he found that he read in haste and without real comprehension, so he postponed his task until his return from the Willig.

He drove past the Willig once and then came back slowly, and it was like seeing it again for the first time. Why did he find it sad that it was from such an address that its occupants would leave for another world? Surely there are thousands of worse ways one might spend one's final days on earth, places infinitely less pleasant. Maybe it was just the fact of death he found sad and the Willig made that thought inescapable.

Felicia Schmidt was in her office and as pleased to see him as a compulsive worrier could be. It was thanks to Felicia that the Willig was the pleasant and spotless and cheerful place it was.

"Father Dowling, how are you? Is this an official visit?"

Felicia's blond bouffant hair-do was sprayed as stiff as her uniform, and her glasses lay upon the ample shelf of her bosom. Her eyeglasses seemed somehow upside down as well as heavily sequined, and she rose to greet him with the half-apprehensive air of a Protestant who feared he would shortly begin some strange rite and carry on in a vaguely oriental way. But on this occasion he had not so much as brought the eucharist for his two former parishioners.

"Just a social call, Felicia." He took the chair she indicated. "How are things?"

"Haven't you heard the news about Sally Wise?"

"Tell me."

Felicia's eyes darted past him to the hallway and Father Dowling offered to shut the door.

"If you would, Father. The least we can do is keep this from our guests. Oh, Father, it is unbelievably awful. I wonder if you ever met Sally Wise? A heavy-set girl, dyed hair, but well trained and a most efficient nurse. She was alone in the world, no husband, divorced, and ideally I prefer my nurses to be settled, wives and mothers, perhaps coming back onto the job market now that their families have been raised."

Felicia sounded like a brochure for the Willig Nursing Home.

"I don't mean that Sally was not a mature person. She was. At least I had every reason to think she was. And now this. Killing herself for a younger man."

It would have been interesting to compare Felicia Schmidt's account of the suicide pact with Phil Keegan's. Identical events would doubtless have an entirely different tone as recounted by a detective and by the manager of the nursing home in which Sally Wise had worked.

"Had you ever met the man?"

She pursed her lips, turned her head to one side and inhaled deeply, causing her glasses to rise almost to the level of her chin. "Yes," she whispered. "It turns out I have. The strangest thing."

And strange it was, the man claiming he was writing an article on nursing homes and interviewing Sally in one of the private salons. "Lord knows what they were up to, Father Dowling. Such a ruse. I don't like having such tricks played on me."

Roger Dowling agreed it was an odd way for the young lovers to meet.

"Young?" Felicia's laugh was harsh. "Sally Wise was not young, Father Dowling. She would not have seen thirty-five again, I can assure you of that."

"Older than the man, then?"

"Oh, yes. Years older. It's why I would not have suspected any hanky-panky even though they spent a good part of the afternoon in that salon. What a fool I was."

"There are worse things, Felicia, than smoothing the way for two people in love."

Felicia put on her glasses. "I had no idea you were such a romantic."

Roger Dowling felt he was playing a bit of a ruse on Felicia himself. He could see the magazines on the shelves behind her, providing a clue to the reading she preferred. And the television set in the corner behind him, its sound turned all but off, provided the latest chapter in some soap opera. Maybe Felicia was a bit jealous of her former employee for having introduced into her life some of the machinations of those daytime dramas on television. Thank God, Marie Murkin was not addicted to them. Father Dowling had heard how severely entangled in that flickering nonsense otherwise sensible people became.

Felicia sighed and her bosom settled. "I don't know how I will be able to break this to Laura Spaulding. Sally and she were so close. I suppose I could ask her son-in-law to let her know Sally will not be with us anymore." Felicia daubed at her eye, lifting her glasses with a lacquered nail to do so. "Laura's son-in-law is Howard Downs."

The little woman sat in a florid housecoat in a chair near a window in her room, the television aroar only a few feet from the hassock on which rested her flouncy slippers. She wore large-lensed black framed glasses and Father Dowling felt her eyes on him from the moment he appeared in her doorway. He had declined Felicia Schmidt's offer to introduce him.

"I'm not a Catholic," the woman said.

"Not everyone is."

She laughed. She held a gadget in her hand, a remote-control unit for her television. She depressed a button and the sound of the television stopped.

"Did you see a nurse in the corridor, big girl, funny-looking hair?"

"You'll have to rephrase the question, Mrs. Spaulding. A gentleman couldn't answer that one."

"They told you my name."

"It's on a plaque next to your door."

"That's right."

"My name is Roger Dowling. May I come in?"

"You're a priest?"

"That's right."

"A Catholic priest?"

"Yes."

"There's not much point. I'm Episcopalian. At least I am when people ask me what my religion is."

"I know your son-in-law, Howard."

"He's no Catholic."

Roger Dowling laughed. "No, he isn't."

"Do you know my daughter, Gloria?"

"I never met her."

"I never see her anymore."

There was not much regret, if any, in the old woman's voice, but it seemed sad she did not know her daughter was dead.

"How old are you, Mrs. Spaulding?"

"Guess."

"Twenty-nine?"

She giggled like a girl but Roger did not feel condescension. Who is so old as to be immune to vanity?

"That's the year I got married. Nineteen twenty-nine. And then the stock market crashed." She smiled faintly. "That was my husband's joke. Actually he did very well during the Depression. Some people did."

"So I've heard. Are you a native of Fox River?"

"Heavens, no." And as she explained that she was from Libertyville ("Where Adlai Stevenson lived"), Father Dowling sensed he was hearing a denial she had repeated through the long years she had lived in Fox River.

It was easy after that; whenever she fell silent a little prod with a question got her going again, and a whole life began to form there in the room, a life more interesting by far than those that continued to flicker on the television screen. Roger Dowling was acquiring a sense of the Willig Nursing Home as a place where silent television is in vogue. Maybe Sally Wise had listened to the old woman like this. If so, she would be missed.

Laura's voice trailed away and that was Roger Dowling's clue they were not alone.

The man in the doorway was as large a man as Father Dowling had ever seen.

25

AFTER HOURS, the Downs Agency had always seemed a pleasant place, almost cozy, but when Michelle returned to it that night after a quick supper to keep the little promise she had made in church, it did not seem a welcoming place.

On previous such returns, as often as not, Gene Lane was there too and that had made a great difference. Now, with Gene so sadly dead, his absence made the agency seem emptier, darker, almost hostile.

Michelle let herself in, turned on the lights embedded in the ceiling over her desk, hung up her coat, and considered turning on all the lights in order to drive away the gloom. But that would have been wasteful, and now that she had been promoted to take over for Phyllis Whitmore, Michelle was not disposed to run up agency expenses. Not that she had ever been profligate, but now it would have been money out of her own pocket.

She opened the door and flicked on the lights in Phyllis's office — when would she begin to think of it as her own? — and then went down the hall and turned on the light in Gene Lane's office. From the doorway, she looked around the room. Why did she feel like an intruder?

How neat Gene had been. Both his desk top and the table behind his desk were models of organization. To the right of his chair, where others had a typewriter, stood the personal computer to which Gene had devoted so much time. And rightly so.

The promise that had brought her here tonight propelled Michelle briskly across the room. She sat at Gene's desk and turned on the computer. While it warmed up, she rotated back and forth in the chair, trying to convince herself that this was the most natural thing in the world, to return here after hours, come into Gene Lane's office, and review his computerization of the agency files.

The computer beside her made a series of noises, indicating that it was ready. Was she? Michelle had not so much as looked at a computer since graduating. Gene, of course, had an array of instructional books and manuals, boxed, all in a row on the table. Michelle opened the one entitled General Operations and settled down to reacquaint herself with the mysteries of the microcomputer.

Gene kept his diskettes in a plastic file on the table, and predictably they were carefully labeled and numbered. He had taken the manufacturer's suggestion and produced back-up disks of all the data he had stored and this brought his little hoard to twenty-four disks. The specter of erasing hours and hours of work, or having it accidentally erased by a power failure, was a diminishing one now, with technical advances, but duplication still was a wise measure.

Michelle inserted a disk entitled DA-DATA into the drive. Its abbreviated title turned out to mean Downs Agency Data. In it Gene had laid down the principles of entering data, in effect writing a handbook for the software program he had devised to pursue his task. Interesting. Michelle removed the disk and replaced it with one intriguingly entitled DADA. This was the beginning of the encoded program that would enable her to draw data from the disk in the second drive.

Within minutes, Michelle was engrossed in the material. The possible combinations of data seemed infinite. What salesman had sold the most home-owners policies in the period from January to June 1978? How many actual claims had been made against those policies and how had they been adjudicated? What was the median age of the purchaser of such policies and how many of them were currently active? These and similar questions the computer answered immediately and with a self-satisfied murmur. The beauty of what Gene had done was obvious, and Michelle felt even worse for failing to encourage him and to champion his project against the skeptical indifference of Howard Downs. When Howard saw how useful the results of Gene's work would be for the agency, he would be as repentant as she was.

Remembering the surprising emergence of her mother as beneficiary of Gloria Downs's life insurance, Michelle typed Yolande Moran and entered it. To her stunned surprise a list of policy numbers appeared on the screen. It seemed clear that there were bugs in Gene's program. But Michelle called up one of the policies and there was her mother's name. Was that totally surprising, given that she had also been a beneficiary of Gloria Downs's policy? It had been taken out many years ago, twenty-three years ago, to be exact, and oddly enough the salesman had been Casimir Janski. Michelle replaced the policy data with the list of policies in which, according to Gene Lane, her mother was listed as beneficiary.

And there she was, plain as day, in the data for each policy as Michelle called it onto the screen, and in most of the cases Howard Downs had been the agent. In the rest it was Janski again. Puzzled, Michelle went through each of the policies carefully and further oddities emerged. The current average age of the insured persons who named her mother as beneficiary was between 75 and 80. Furthermore, in a number of them there was a primary and second beneficiary and in these her mother was always named second. Listed first in those, invariably, was Laura Spaulding.

Michelle entered Laura Spaulding's name and a list longer than that conjured up by her mother's name appeared. She went through several of these, coming to a policy on Howard Downs himself, the most modest amount of any policy thus far. Laura Spaulding, his secondary beneficiary after his wife, was identified as his mother-in-law.

Howard's mother-in-law? Good Lord. Michelle asked the machine how much money had been paid to Laura Spaulding as beneficiary of policies sold by the Downs Agency and stared unbelievingly at an amount in excess of nine million dollars. Surely such an outlay of cash would have been noticed by the insurer! But when she checked, she saw why this had not happened. Only two of the policies in which Laura Spaulding was listed as beneficiary were held by the same company and one of these was the modest one on Howard Downs's life. What did it all mean?

It made little sense to name an elderly woman the beneficiary of so many policies, particularly when she had already received an astronomical amount of benefits. Even if Howard could have been so enamored of his wife's mother — which, given the tension between him and Gloria, seemed unlikely — why would Casimir Janski have sold so many policies in which Laura was the beneficiary? It wasn't as if either agent benefited from all this.

Or was it?

Michelle sat transfixed by the screen, calling up before her wondering eye more and more elements of the data Gene Lane had entered, asking for more and different permutations and combinations of the data. Rather than diminish, her bewilderment grew. Finally, she got a listing of policy numbers and the holders of the policies in which either her mother or Laura Spaulding figured and printed them out. She tore the perforated pages from the printer and folded them carefully before putting them into her purse. She did not have the faintest idea why she wanted them or what she intended to do with them.

After she turned off the microcomputer and replaced the diskettes in their file, Michelle doused the lights in Gene's office. The room was at the side of the building and its window looked out on the lighted parking lot that served the agency as well as a small clinic. How lonely her car looked parked out there.

As she stood by the window, a set of headlights swept across the lot and then a large luxury car purred over the blacktop and into the place next to Michelle's car. The door opened and Casimir Janski emerged. He eased the driver's door closed, glanced toward the agency building, and then bent to look into her car. Michelle did not know if Janski would recognize her vehicle. She could hardly blame him for being surprised to find someone at the agency at this hour. Her watch read ten-thirty, a time hard to believe, but it testified to how absorbed she had been in the computer and its surprising revelations.

When Janski let himself in the front door, Michelle had already come out of Gene Lane's office. The sight of her visibly surprised Janski and for a moment she felt menace in his reaction. But then he relaxed.

"Oh, it's you. I saw the light on in Phyllis's office. Is that your car in the lot?"

Michelle nodded and the universe seemed to become devoid of mystery again for Casimir Janski.

"Howard has given me Phyl's office."

"Good idea."

His eyes went to Gene Lane's door. Did he wonder why she was closer to Gene's office than she was to Phyllis's? The memory of Janski's name forming in green letters on the computer monitor, a list that seemed to track past her mind's eye, on and on and on, did not prompt her to ask him any of the questions that had been occurring to her in the past several hours. If he had been startled to find her here, she was still somewhat frightened by the menace he had momentarily threatened when he first saw her. She did not want to learn what his reaction might be to finding out she had a list of curious policies for which he had been the agent.

"You been moving into the new office, or what?"

"Oh, no. I had some work to do."

He had taken his coat off and laid it carefully over his arm. "What kind of work?"

She looked at him, unable to think of a lie.

He repeated his question: "What work were you doing?"

She managed a sort of laugh. "Nothing important. It could have waited. You're right. Mainly, I just wanted to see my new office and let my imagination have free rein."

He considered her answer and for a moment she feared he would reject it as implausible.

"What brings you back so late?" she asked.

It was his turn to think of an answer.

"I was driving past and saw the lights on."

Michelle had the feeling that they had just exchanged lies. Any notion that she could remove the mystery of what she had found by talking of it with Mr. Janski, or with Howard Downs, was gone. But she had to talk about it with someone.

The realization that this was the sort of problem she would quite naturally have gone to Gene Lane with brought a lump to her throat. For the first time she wondered if his death had anything to do with what she had found on his computer.

She did not bother to lock the door when she went out. Let Mr. Janski take care of it. She slid into her car, started the motor, and backed out of her place.

Somewhere between the office door and her car she realized she was on her way to see Father Dowling.

26

MICHELLE MORAN came to him without a very clear idea of the purpose of her visit, but then she did not yet have a clear understanding of what she had discovered in Gene Lane's computerization of the records of the Downs Agency.

"Does your mother know any of these insured people?"

"I doubt it. For that matter, it was surprising that she was the beneficiary of Mrs. Downs's policy, but in that case there was at least a far-fetched explanation. They had known each other, after all."

"And Howard Downs is a benefactor of your family."

She nodded in assent to that, but it gave her some small pain to do so. Clearly, she was beginning to have doubts about the man who had treated her like a father all these years.

Father Dowling said, "Why do you suppose he has been so good to you and your mother?"

She placed the tip of a finger on the point of her chin and looked at him. She spoke softly. "I used to imagine they would marry."

"Your mother and Howard Downs?"

"Yes."

"Then he would be your father."

"That is how I've always thought of him."

"Maybe there is a reason for that."

"What do you mean?"

"It would certainly explain his concern for your mother and you if he really were your father."

But Michelle saw this only as a flight of fancy. "I suppose. Maybe a real father wouldn't be as nice."

"What was your own father like?"

"I never knew him."

"He died when you were young?"

"He died before I was even born."

"Ah."

He had given her a cup of coffee but she had scarcely touched it. Now, when she did taste it, she quickly put it down again. "Would you like me to warm that up?"

"I really don't want it, Father."

"Could I get you something else?"

But her mind was still pursuing the train of thought he had suggested. She said musingly, "It would have been possible, I suppose. They were always close. But that means..."

Did it shock her to think she was the child of their sin? Roger Dowling could not bring himself to tell Michelle what André Conway had told him. That would be to assume too great a responsibility, to be the vehicle of such earth-shaking news. He was playing with fire now in providing Michelle with the occasion to come to the realization on her own. Maybe she could have called up on Gene Lane's computer the date of her father's death. She would not have to be told the date of her own birth.

But it was not simply the possible emotional shock to her that prevented Roger Dowling from telling Michelle she was the daughter of Howard Downs. What she had told him of her findings on the computer had suddenly seemed to provide the missing explanation of recent events. He suspected that Michelle was simply blocking from her mind the truth that the ultimate gainer from the policies that she had learned of from the computer,

■ 168 ■

those of which Laura Spaulding or Yolande Moran were beneficiaries, was none other than Howard Downs.

And Casimir Janski.

The appearance of the giant senior associate of the Downs
Agency in the doorway of Laura Spaulding's room at the Willig
Nursing Home had had a sobering effect on the old lady. Janski
was gone almost as soon as he appeared, backing away with an
embarrassed wave of his hand at the priest. But Laura Spaulding
had seen him and she leaned close to Father Dowling.

"I don't like that man. I never did."

"Isn't he an associate of your son-in-law?"

"I still don't like him. I told Sally to keep clear of him, but
when has a young woman ever listened to her elders? But I guess
nothing came of it."

"Mr. Janski was interested in Sally Wise?"

"Do you know her?"

"One of the nurses here?" he said carefully. It gave an unwelcome sense of power to know that Laura's daughter and her
nurse were dead and the old woman was still unaware of it.

"Sally is interested in him. Or she was. He left her in the
lurch. Now I suppose he is coming back."

Felicia Schmidt had known nothing of any dating between
Sally Wise and Casimir Janski. It was possible the old woman had
imagined things, perhaps by teasing her nurse and then coming
to believe her own teasing. But after he had spoken to Michelle,
Roger Dowling no longer doubted Laura.

And then Michelle mentioned Janski's coming to the agency
that night.

"I gave him a bit of a shock, I guess. He saw a light on in
Phyllis Whitmore's office."

"That would be a shock."

"Well, he frightened me too."

"Did you tell him what you had found on the computer?"

She frowned as she shook her head. "No. And then I came directly here."

"Do you happen to know Howard Downs's telephone number?"

She did. When he began to dial it she asked, somewhat alarmed, what he was doing. The phone was already ringing in his ear when he told her it seemed best to clear up the mystery of all those insurance policies. Downs answered the phone in an irritated voice but professed to be pleased to hear from Father Dowling when the priest identified himself.

"I wonder if you will still say that when I ask if you could possibly come here to the rectory?"

"Any time, Father."

"In half an hour?"

"Tonight!"

"I know this is late to be calling, but Michelle and I have been talking and..."

"Michelle is there with you?"

"That's right."

He said he would come. It was after eleven-thirty when Roger Dowling made the call. Immediately he put through two more, the first to Phil Keegan, the second to Cy Horvath.

"I'm already in bed, Roger."

"Well, call me in the morning then. I think I have the explanation of all these recent deaths."

"Cut it out, Roger."

"Michelle Moran is here with me now. Howard Downs is on his way."

"What has happened?"

"Michelle Moran discovered the missing middle term."

She gave him a frowning smile after he hung up. "Do you really believe that?"

"Of course I do."

"Father, you shouldn't jump to conclusions. What I told you, what I found out on the computer, well, there isn't necessarily anything wrong. Sure, it's surprising. I admit that I am a little bit shocked that my mother and Mrs. Spaulding should show up as beneficiaries on so many policies. But that doesn't mean anybody has done anything wrong. And what does it have to do with those deaths?"

"Don't you think it has something to do with Gene Lane's dying?"

"How could it? They say he committed suicide."

"Yes. A suicide pact with a woman he didn't even know."

"Maybe he did know her. How much did I really know about Gene Lane's life?"

"Well, why don't we wait until the others arrive?"

27

IT WAS a little snug in the rectory study with Michelle and Howard Downs and Phil Keegan occupying all the chairs on the far side of the desk. Father Dowling looked up from the computer print-outs laid before him. His eyes met Howard Downs.

"Howard, earlier Michelle and I were speaking of your extraordinary concern for the well-being of her family. Of her mother and herself."

"Because Gloria remembered Yolande in her insurance policy?" Downs's brow lifted but his expression did not alter. "Years ago, when I started out as an independent agent, Yolande's husband was my partner. He died and I made certain that Yolande continued to profit from her husband's interest in the agency."

"Out of revenues?"

Downs moved his head back and the corners of his mouth dimpled. "Out of revenues, yes. Is that why you wanted this clandestine meeting, to discuss the affairs of the Downs Agency?" He turned to Keegan. "Captain, you will find what I have just said, and more, in the records of endless interviews I have had with your minions."

"And wimions," Michelle said loyally. "Don't forget Officer Lamb."

"Are there other ways that you channel money to Michelle's mother, Howard?"

"I've helped her in various ways over the years. I haven't kept records of everything. I didn't think of it as tax deductible." It was the first time Roger Dowling had detected a righteous note in Howard's voice.

"But your agency has kept very thorough records over the years. Records that one of your younger associates has entered into a computer."

Downs nodded. "Eugene Lane. Yes." He shook his head. "Honest to God, these have been strange months. My wife, Phyllis, Gene..." He looked at Michelle and Roger Dowling thought the young woman would go to comfort the man she did not realize was her father. The way she glanced at the pieces of paper on the desk suggested she now regretted having brought them here and precipitated this late-night meeting at the rectory. Well, it was too late for regrets now.

"Your records can now be consulted with amazing facility. When they are, they reveal that your mother-in-law and Yolande Moran are beneficiaries of an extraordinary number of policies."

"What do you mean?"

For answer, Roger Dowling selected one of the sheets of paper and handed it to Howard. His eye traveled down the list, pausing halfway—but only someone watching his eyes would have noticed—continued to the end, and tossed the paper back onto the desk.

"Are you suggesting there is some irregularity?"

"Are you suggesting there is nothing surprising about the fact that your mother-in-law is the beneficiary of policies worth well over nine million dollars, policies drawn on different companies and written on the lives of people it would be surprising to learn hold your mother-in-law in such esteem?"

"I have no intention of discussing the affairs of my agency at such a meeting as this." Again he turned to Phil Keegan. "Was this meeting your idea, Captain?"

"I'm a guest here like everyone else," Keegan growled. "A thirsty guest."

This provided a diversion, with Phil going to the kitchen for beer and running into Marie Murkin who shagged him back into the study. In a moment she arrived to take orders, casting one coldly accusative glance at the pastor. The idea, having a house full of people without even informing the housekeeper! Father Dowling was the only one willing to risk coffee at this time of night. Downs and Keegan had beer and Michelle a glass of white wine.

"Downs is right," Phil said, when they were once more settled. "What has all this got to do with the death of his wife, or of Phyllis Whitmore, or of Vincent Arthur Farrell?"

"Or of Sally Wise and Gene Lane?" Roger Dowling added.

"I certainly can't be said to have killed all those people. I mean, how could I have?"

"That is hardly an insurmountable problem, Howard. One does not have to perform the actual murder in order to be a murderer. One can employ instruments, surrogates."

Howard Downs looked shocked. "I thought you were my friend, Father."

Howard Downs was not alone in wanting to know the justification for Father Dowling's implication. Michelle had definitely changed her mind now and allied herself with Downs. She even moved her chair closer to his, but that did not alter the fact that it was she who had brought the computer print-outs to the rectory. When Howard realized Michelle had provided the basis for his downfall, who knew what he would do? Phil Keegan asked what Downs's motive was supposed to be.

"After the wife, I mean. Why the others?"

Again the priest indicated the papers on his desk. "Money. Howard will turn out to be the sole heir of the estate of Laura Spaulding. The millions of dollars that have already gone to her and the millions more slated for her are ultimately destined for Howard Downs. The same can be said of the money going to Michelle's mother. Would you care to explain that, Howard?"

"I wouldn't want to interrupt."

"Is there anything you want to tell Michelle?"

The look that Downs gave Michelle was fleeting, but filled with apprehension. Nothing that had happened to Howard since Father Dowling had met the man had pierced him as genuinely as this.

"Tell her what?" he croaked, fumbling with his pack of cigarettes.

Father Dowling waited, but when Howard did not speak, he said, "Michelle and I were discussing earlier the interval between her father's death and her own birth. Do you know when Michelle's father died?"

In the end he did not have to make a dramatic announcement. Howard Downs turned to Michelle and she with a little agonized cry read the message in his tortured eyes. He took her in his arms and the two of them wept. Phil Keegan blew his nose, sipped his beer, and glared at the priest for getting him into a sentimental mess like this. The ringing of the doorbell came like a reprieve.

"Would you get that, Phil? Please."

Keegan was up and well on his way to the door before Marie Murkin could come from her kitchen. It was just as well. A moment later Keegan brought Casimir Janski into the study.

The huge man stood beside Keegan. He looked at the priest, at the papers on his desk top, he looked at Michelle and Howard Downs still clinging to each other with tears in their eyes. With a sudden movement he pushed Phil into a corner of the room, catching him by surprise. A gun appeared in his hand as if by magic. Then he disarmed a glowering Phil Keegan.

■ 175 ■

"All right. Everybody sit down. Howard, bring me up to date on the proceedings thus far."

"How did you know I was here?"

Janski grinned. "You may be a damned fool, Howard, but I'm not. Michelle, you were in Lane's office tonight, weren't you? I could feel that his computer was still warm."

"Did you follow me here?"

"Not quite. You got away pretty fast. What has she told them, Howard?"

"Father Dowling has been doing the explaining, Casey, not I."

"He figured it out?"

"Figured what out!" Keegan roared. His face was black with fury at having been so easily disarmed. The thought that he was being held hostage, and in the St. Hilary rectory, was doing dangerous things to his blood pressure. But it was Michelle's reaction that Father Dowling watched for. Downs could not conceal from his daughter that awful revelations were in the offing.

The priest spoke. "Mr. Janski and Howard Downs have been partners of a darker sort for many years. I suspect that a more thorough search into the records of the Downs Agency will show that Janski has been feathering his nest in the same way Howard has." Again he held up the computer print-outs.

"I'm not worried about any computer," Janski said. "I took care of that tonight."

And now he had come to take care of other loose ends. Seated where he was, behind his desk, Father Dowling was the only one who saw Cy Horvath when he appeared in the hall.

Horvath sized up the situation without showing the least surprise or excitement. His gun was in his hand. He brought it down hard on Janski's head as he moved into the room. Keegan sprang from the corner and grabbed Janski's arm as if they had practiced this many times. The gun flew from Janski's hand and skidded along the floor to Howard's feet.

Did he even for a moment dream of picking it up and making a break for freedom? Freedom. And where was that?

Howard Downs looked at Michelle, kicked the gun away, under the desk, and slumped in his chair.

28

SEVERAL DAYS later Phil Keegan was having lunch with Roger Dowling at the St. Hilary rectory when Marie Murkin joined them at the dining-room table and said she still could not understand what Casimir Janski had done.

"Done!" Keegan glared at her, not without affection. "The man killed Mrs. Downs, Farrell, Phyllis Whitmore, Sally Wise, and Gene Law." He ticked the victims off on his huge fingers before leaning toward the housekeeper. "And, my dear, two nights ago he might have killed you too, right in this house."

Whether because of the term of endearment or the shivering prospect of being at the center of Phil Keegan's attention, Marie giggled with ambiguous pleasure.

"Oh, don't be silly. I was in no more danger than you were."

"That's what I mean."

"It's true, Marie," the pastor said. "If Cy Horvath had not arrived when he did, Janski might have added us all to his list of victims."

Keegan sat back and his frown deepened at this reminder of how his lieutenant had saved them all. He continued to blame himself mercilessly for having been disarmed by Janski, and Father Dowling's suggestion that this was all for the best ("We wouldn't have wanted a shootout in the rectory, Phil") did not console him. Marie did a better job of that now by turning the conversation to the complicated topic of Janski's motive for killing all those people.

Lighting his pipe, puffing up great clouds of contemplative smoke, Father Dowling thought that understanding the scheme to defraud as much as he himself now did helped somewhat to make Howard Downs's previous actions less mysterious. Michelle had helped the priest puzzle it out, her tone of disbelief tinged with a trace of grudging respect for the technical accomplishment of the scheme.

It would have been difficult to tell, apart from Howard Downs's lengthy statement to the police, whether the two men had entered into the plan together or — Downs's version — Janski had started it independently and, when discovered by Downs, had forced his partner into an illegal partnership by pointing out what the adverse publicity his own exposure would do to the agency. Once in, permitting a reluctant toe to try the illicit waters, Downs had rapidly been knee-deep in wrongdoing. At first, it had been easy.

"It was easy until Gloria," Downs said, lighting another cigarette. Father Dowling reflected that he had seen the man more frequently imprisoned than free and this time it was most unlikely that he would escape prolonged punishment. "What we were doing seemed almost innocent. A name on a piece of paper, a possibility of fraud in an indefinite future." Downs smiled sardonically as he dragged on his cigarette. "Embezzlement is an antiseptic crime, Father Dowling. You need never touch real money. It's just a matter of entries, a shift of figures or names. Nowadays you can do it long distance by computers. Computers. I wouldn't be here today if I hadn't okayed that computer for Gene Lane."

Michelle did not contest her father's claim. "I suppose they could have gotten away with it. At least they could have if they hadn't been so greedy. Eventually it would have caught up with them. It was relatively simple to conceal those secondary beneficiaries from the insured. I doubt that most of them saw the final policy. The agency offers to keep them secure. Companies are another matter, and Gene wasn't the only one who uses computers. Companies merge, their records are combined in the same computer, and it would be just a matter of time before someone saw the same beneficiaries showing up on different policies."

Michelle spoke as if hoping it were true. The fact was she was almost relieved her father had been arrested.

"Now what he did, bad as it was, can be separated from the horrors Janski committed."

Downs was adamant and believable in insisting he had had nothing to do with any of those deaths.

"Directly, I mean. I don't pretend to total innocence of them. I killed no one and I had no idea that Janski intended to. But he couldn't wait for nature to make us rich. He had to kill to hurry the process along."

"But why your wife?"

Pain flickered across Downs's face. "Yes. My wife. That was a stroke of genius on Casey's part. He knew Gloria and I didn't get along. Here was a way to make me a closer accomplice and tie my hands once and for all. When I discovered Gloria, I was so stunned I didn't connect it with our fraudulent scheme. I thought Phyllis Whitmore had done it." Downs glanced at the priest. "How hellish this must sound to you."

Roger Dowling preferred to relate the events to purgatory. *The Divine Comedy* was among his three favorite books and Downs was indeed right in thinking of the glutinous events that had dragged him deeper and deeper into trouble in Dantesque terms. Gustave Doré illustrations came and went in the priest's mind, but it was Janski, not Downs, he could imagine up to his

■ 180 ■

neck in ice in the lowest region of the inferno. However mixed his motives, Downs's willingness to go on trial for his wife's murder when he thought Phyllis Whitmore had done it possessed a note of nobility.

"Why was Farrell killed?"

"The poor fool. He guessed my reason for not defending myself and for being of no help to him. Phyllis. That would have been all right, but then he wondered if there weren't a further motive. He made the fatal mistake of asking Janski how profitable to me Gloria's death would be."

"And Janski panicked?"

"That is not the word I would use. He calculated rather than panicked. He felt that Farrell's understandable curiosity—the man would wonder what kind of bill he could stick me with—could be the beginning of questions that might reveal what we had been up to. I should have suspected Casey's involvement when he was the one to telephone me that Farrell had been murdered. How did he know? I was so ready to believe Phyllis responsible, I didn't even think of that. And he himself was counting heavily on money from policies taken out on Gloria."

Janski, in anticipation of all the promissory wealth buried in the files of the Downs Agency, had gone heavily into the market and was constantly juggling margin calls. Perhaps he dreamed of getting rich legitimately, but his bad luck in the market aggravated his need for money. It was a fleetingly pleasant thought that Janski had wanted to extract himself from the web he had woven. So far, Janski had refused to see Father Dowling, but of course the priest meant to persist in his efforts to talk to the man the Fox River *Messenger* described as a mass murderer.

Mervel was at his self-righteous best writing about these gory events, and Ninian of the *Tribune* was not far behind. They seemed to wax eloquent with the realization that they themselves had neither the temptation nor the opportunity to kill five people. "Five that we know about," added Gert Fingeret in the *Fox River Shopper*, where she approached the case through an astrological analysis of the principals. Bruce Wiggins looked soulfully into the camera and wondered aloud to his viewers whether the case did not represent a death blow to capitalism. "Or however we wish to characterize the economics of greed," he read, the words those of a disgruntled copywriter who had missed winning the Illinois Lottery by one digit.

It was a curious thought, that greed is a function of one economic system rather than another. Father Dowling found he did not share the widely expressed incredulity at what Casimir Janski had done. Downs had been right about the nature of money. There is a severe limit on what anyone can buy or use, so wealth must remain an abstract possibility, numbers on a sheet, certificates in a box, some precious metal in a vault. The image of the miser running gold coins through his gnarled fingers is inherently implausible. Who can love money in its physical state?

"I love the look of French banknotes," Michelle said. "Especially the ten-franc note."

"But would you want a million of them cluttering up your room?"

Michelle looked dubious, so Father Dowling changed the subject. The point he was making, if only to himself, was that Janski did not kill Gloria Downs or anyone else because he was enamored of a stack of dollar bills. She had been a means, as the others had been a threat, to his abstract desire for wealth.

"Which he probably could not define."

"Look, Roger," Phil Keegan said. "Two pretty shrewd guys were involved in fraud. Both of them wanted to be rich and don't ask me to define it either. Only one of them killed a lot of people in order to make sure he would get the money. Whatever the difference, it is an important one. The difference between maybe ten years and life."

Father Dowling dropped it. He would have had better luck with Phil than with Michelle developing the thought that anyone could very easily find himself in circumstances where he would do as much bad or more than Casimir Janski. Even Ninian and Mervel and Gert Fingeret. Bruce Wiggins was already committing a crime the way he did the local news. For the priest, the great difference between both Downs and Janski and their victims was that the two insurance agents could still repent of what they had done.

In the Mass he said at noon in St. Hilary's, Father Dowling now remembered the victims of Casimir Janski, praying for the repose of their souls. Gloria Downs. Phyllis Whitmore. The feckless Farrell. Poor Sally Wise who had made Janski nervous and sealed her fate when she agreed to lure Gene Lane to his doom. She could scarcely be allowed to go on living, knowing how Gene Lane had died.

Arraignments took place, court dates were set, eventually the horrible events faded from the news. For the nonce. Michelle, who would face the task of seeing the agency through this difficult period and getting it off to a new start, left for Florida and a few weeks with her mother. Mrs. Moran did not come north when news of the father of her child came to her. It made far more sense that Michelle should go to her mother than that her mother should come to her.

"I seem fated to be a career woman," she said wistfully to Father Dowling when she came to say good-by.

"Maybe you will meet some Lothario in Florida."

"At the moment, the thought of taking over the agency is more attractive."

Watching Michelle go out to her car, he murmured a prayer for her. Her entrance into the world had been by an unusual route and her passage through it had been bumpy. Thank God that her father, now that she had found him, was not guilty of more serious crimes.

At the Willig Nursing Home, Father Dowling sat in a parlor with Mrs. Spaulding but failed to have a conversation. The little old woman worked her denture, her white hair was fluffy, and her eyes seemed clear and wary. From time to time they flashed with an almost malicious glint. He spoke to her of her daughter and he spoke of Sally Wise as well, on the theory that if her mind was working the old lady should know of these deaths, and if it was not, the information could do no harm. Her lack of response was daunting, but rather than stop, he was prompted into a lengthy monologue. He recounted for Mrs. Spaulding the scheme her son-in-law and Casimir Janski had been engaged in. She seemed to follow what he was saying.

"So you are rich, Mrs. Spaulding. Very rich."

She laughed. A brief, barking laugh. Then she closed in upon herself again, returning to real or feigned senility.

The sound of her laugh stayed with him as he walked out to his car.

It would do, he thought, it would more than do, as a commentary on the events of the past weeks.

c.